To Cih
ho.
Co

x
26·6·93

Night's Black Agents

Clifford Benyon, landlord of the grandiosely named Belle Vue Hotel in the Birmingham district of Ladywood, is tortured by his wife's flagrant affair with Thomas Beech, a traveller in surgical supplies and one of the hotel's regular and free-spending customers.

In despair, Benyon contracts with the brutal canal boatman, Ezra Talbot, to kill his rival.

The deed is duly done, but its results are far from what Benyon had hoped. Not only does his wife retreat ever further from him, but it brings Detective-Inspector John Hammond on the scene. And Hammond has an intuitive grasp of the truth of the affair. The only problem is: can he prove it?

As events unfold, Benyon is horrified to find that the crime he has initiated is developing its own terrifying momentum.

Set on the canals of the Midlands and North-West during the 1930s, David Armstrong's first novel is an atmospheric, character-based mystery which intrigues as much by its unusual background as by the cat-and-mouse game played out between police and murderer.

DAVID ARMSTRONG

Night's Black Agents

Good things of day begin to droop and drowse,
Whiles night's black agents to their preys do rouse.
Macbeth

THE CRIME CLUB
An Imprint of HarperCollins *Publishers*

First published in Great Britain in 1993
by The Crime Club, an imprint of
HarperCollinsPublishers, 77–85 Fulham Palace Road,
Hammersmith, London W6 8JB

9 8 7 6 5 4 3 2 1

David Armstrong asserts the moral right to be identified
as the author of this work.

A catalogue record for this book is
available from the British Library

ISBN 0 00 232431 8

Photoset in Linotron Baskerville by
Rowland Phototypesetting Ltd
Bury St Edmunds, Suffolk
Printed and bound in Great Britain by
HarperCollins Book Manufacturing, Glasgow

For my Mother and Father

PROLOGUE

The boy walked the horse up the sandy slope beside the
tunnel's entrance. He moved slowly, didn't want the walk
to end, feared it, knew what the next thing would be.

Below him, on the smooth water, the boat rocked very
slightly. The horse missed its footing, scraped at the sandy
soil to regain it, and the boy started with fear.

On he went, the heat filling his brow with dirty sweat
that ran down into his eyes and stung him. He beat at the
nettles with his stick as he climbed.

At the top he crossed the metalled lane in the shade of
the still ash trees and took the path. Fifty feet beneath
him, cut through the sandstone, was the black tunnel. He
smacked at the fern and bracken that threatened to over-
whelm the narrow path.

And then they were ready to descend. The horse's back
rocked from side to side as it made its ungainly progress
down the incline towards the tunnel's exit.

The boy tied the horse's rein to a mooring post at the
tunnel's dark mouth and started the walk back up and over
the hill.

His father had made ready their lying planks and, as the
boy approached, he stepped from the boat and hauled its
great weight up to the tunnel.

'All right?' he said.

The boy said nothing, but stepped aboard and lay down
on his back, grasping the rough plank. His father eased the
boat into the gaping blackness and then lay down on the
other side.

And so it began: the man and the boy 'legging' the boat

through the tunnel, pushing the brick sides with their boots and easing the hulk through its blackness in stealth and quiet.

The boy glanced back and saw the ring of light shrinking as they made their terrible progress. His legs were barely long enough to reach the slippery brick sides. His father, with one steady push, covered the distance that the boy strove to make in two or three strides. But he struggled to keep their rhythm, and he gave all the strength that his legs could muster.

The boat made eerie progress through the still water, leaving a little swirl in its wake. Drips from the roof fell echoing to the surface; the only other sounds the heavy breathing of the man, the short, frightened breaths of the boy.

Now the boy inclined his head to the right and saw the pinhole of hope at the other end.

He pushed hard and his boot slipped on the slimy wall. Before he could regain his grip he was falling into the space between boat and wall. And then, even as the black water covered him and filled his screaming mouth, he felt his leg being crushed between the tunnel wall and the boat.

He knew that this was his death. It was cold and he opened his mouth to protest, and the water came in and no sound emerged.

Something brushed him, and then again, and suddenly he was lifted with great power out of the water.

He lay shivering in the rudder space and the last thing he heard was his father clawing the boat along, moving from side to side and using his hands and his feet to propel them towards the light.

He was in a lorry or a van. He lay on the floor, a blanket or sack around him. There was straw and a smell of animals. But he was out of the blackness. His leg was in great pain and he began to sob quietly.

They took him into the hospital and soon his father was gone, back to the boat.

In this strange world, nurses and doctors came and went and sometimes spoke to him, but they received no response. The boy ate and lay in bed. They explained something to him about his leg and then put him to sleep.

He couldn't feel his leg at all the next day and then, when the feeling came back, he was in great pain. The pain grew and grew, and he had no notion of when it would stop. He cried quietly and secretly.

Days later, when he was allowed to walk to the lavatory, it was with sticks to help him. He hobbled along and they watched him closely.

When his father returned they explained to him that the boy's leg had been so badly crushed that they had had to operate to save it. He would now walk with a caliper, a metal splint, but it would not hinder him. He had been very lucky.

They thought that the boy should not have been doing this man's work, but there was no point in saying so. He was one of thousands on the waterways: children who had no education and whose lives were in constant danger. Only God knew how many were maimed. It was a world apart.

They told him that it was lucky that he had been so close to a hospital. And that a farmer had brought them here so quickly, otherwise the boy could have died. The man said nothing. He asked only when the boy could leave. Six weeks. In about six weeks he would be fitted with his caliper and would be able to leave.

The boy watched him go. On the stiff card at the end of the iron bed was the boy's name, Ezra Talbot.

CHAPTER 1

Ezra walked through Hockley, up Constitution Hill, past Snow Hill station and out the other side of Birmingham towards the wharf at Nechells. It was the first week of July 1933.

His lad was there. There was no affection in the term. William had worked a flight of locks for him, unbidden, several years ago, when Ezra's father had been dying of pneumonia in the cabin below. William was surly and silent, but he knew how to take a boat through a flight of locks and, as they cleared the last one, he had looked at Ezra who sat at the tiller, and stepped tentatively aboard. He had been with him ever since.

They were ideal company. Ezra had no wish for conversation; William had none. They simply worked, ate and, when on the move, slept on board together; but there was no human warmth between them. William had no idea where Ezra spent his time ashore, and Ezra couldn't have been less interested what William did with his. If the man had a second name, Ezra didn't know it. Had Ezra's not been painted on the side of the cabin, William probably wouldn't have known his either.

William was leaning against the wall of one of the wharfside offices, a single-storey, red-brick building that dealt with paperwork for the owners and carriers; loads, weights, cargoes and tolls. He looked insolent, and he sucked on the back of his throat and fetched up phlegm which he gobbed on to the greasy water in front of him. A trickle of saliva stayed on his bottom lip. The laces of his muddy black boots were undone. Ezra acknowledged him with a nod and, as he passed him, said, 'Any word yet?'

'I ain't seen anyone,' said William without moving or uncrossing his legs. Ezra went into the office.

A few minutes later he came out and walked towards the narrow boat. The younger man moved behind him. 'They ain't got a load here yet. Reckon it could be all day, maybe tomorrow. He said I'd do better at Icknield. We'll go down there. Get the horse.'

William ambled off to the stables while Ezra stepped aboard the boat, unlocked the cabin and started to man- œuvre the huge rudder into a position where the two men could hang it into its bracket.

When the big grey Shire was harnessed and the rudder dropped in, Ezra cast off and William led away. The slack was picked up and, as the tow rope drew taut, the huge boat made its first jolting move.

It was hard to make a living carrying; it was impossible if you were tied up for days at a time waiting for loads that sometimes never came.

The two men spent the rest of the day loading coal from the siding at Icknield Loop in Hockley. The coal-carrying railway wagons rolled right up to the edge of the cut and tipped their loads directly into the holds of the barges and narrow boats. But it was still hard and dirty work. The load needed to be shovelled down and 'pockets' filled.

Coal was the heaviest, dirtiest and least desirable cargo, but it was always there. There was always coal to be carried.

At seven that evening, with the vessel overloaded and sheeted down against the promised rain, William shuffled away.

Ezra stayed on board and washed the grime from his neck and brow. At nine o'clock he locked the grubby little cabin and walked away from the wharf towards the Belle Vue Hotel in Icknield Port Road. It was called a hotel, but it was just like any other town pub that he drank in. He

didn't even think there were rooms to stay overnight in any
longer. It was a quiet pub and those who stood at the long
bar or sat in small groups at the heavy iron tables were
only interested in their steady, quiet drinking. He sat in the
corner with a pint of dark mild. No one bothered him, and
he spoke to no one.

The name of the licensee over the door was Benyon,
and Clifford Benyon had come to expect the visits of the
big-framed man every two or three weeks. He enjoyed his
solitary, serious drinking: a pint of mild; a pint and a
whisky; another whisky; a half of mild and a double Scotch.

When closing time was called and Ezra walked to the
bar to order a final drink, Clifford raised his hand as he
gave it to him in a gesture that told him there was no need
to hurry.

Ezra thought that he had been accepted into a late drinking group. But one after another, the small groups left.
Now, the only noise came from behind the frosted-glass
and mahogany partition in the smoke-room. Clifford stood
behind the bar, washing glasses and wiping up. Ezra sat
with his drinks in front of him. Clifford looked over to him.
Ezra forced his vacant, unpractised smile. The noise of
laughter came from next door. A woman's voice rose above
the rest. Ezra had seen the customers in there, they were
in suits and spats, every one of them wore a collar; the
landlord's wife served them. He had often seen her walking
through the bar, a good-looking woman of about thirty,
perhaps a little older, who barely acknowledged her husband and hardly looked at the drinkers there. Her business
was elsewhere.

Talbot was a watcher. And this handsome woman had
the bearing of a woman who was more than a wife; her
husband the appearance of a man who is not in full possession of that wife. In particular, Ezra had observed the
familiarity that existed between Mrs Benyon and a dapper

man with a Northern accent who could often be heard above the rest of the company in the smoke-room on almost every occasion that Ezra had found himself in the bar. She stood close to him at the piano when he played. Just that little bit too close, thought Ezra. And once, as he had stood at the bar, he was sure that he had seen their fingers touch for a moment as she had passed him his drinks.

The slow minutes ticked by on the yellowing face of the big clock behind the bar, and Ezra began to feel a little uncomfortable, the drink burdensome rather than welcome. He drank down the beer and gently rolled the whisky around the glass. Clifford caught his eye and called him to the bar.

'Have another,' he said, and, without waiting for an answer, put a fresh tumbler to the bottle of spirits and poured him a generous measure. He also poured himself one.

The huddle of voices from the smoke-room continued. Clifford and Ezra drank assiduously, in part to conceal the dearth of conversation between them. Neither of them had the currency of easy talk. It was at times like these that people made gestures: you gave, you even asked for, it was simply a means of trying to build a bridge of trust. Uncharacteristically, Ezra offered. Out of the blue. There would be something in it for him as well. But there was no need to offer. Men's talk. Conspiratorial, a financial side to it. 'I can get you some rum at the right price if you like,' said Ezra. 'Next trip. Up North. I've got a mate there. A business partner.' He pronounced the last three words slowly, and neither man was convinced by the phrase. He meant he knew a crook. 'I can get as much as you like. Within reason.'

'Within reason,' echoed Clifford. 'How much would it be? How much for a case or two?' He was trying to sound sensible. It was the contact he wanted, not the rum. Of course he'd have the rum. But sound sensible, reasonable to do business with, that was the thing.

'I'll see you when I've got it. The price'll be right, don't worry about that. I'll see you all right.'

'Let's drink to it,' said Clifford, and poured more whisky into their glasses. Then a shriek of laughter came shrill from behind the partition and there was a look of loathing in Clifford's watery brown eyes. Of course, Ezra had been right. The landlord looked at him, and Ezra met his gaze. It was the first time that their eyes had really met. Ill at ease, Ezra looked down at his glass, lifted it to his lips and sucked the spirit down.

Clifford walked him to the door as the laughter from behind the glass welled up again. Ezra slipped through the gap that Clifford made for him. 'Next time,' said the landlord. 'See you next time.'

CHAPTER 2

He was as good as his word. Within the month he walked
through the door of the bar of the Belle Vue and immediately caught Clifford's eye. He signalled with a nod of his
head to the backyard and walked through the bar to the
door that led to the Gents.

Talbot was standing in the shadow of the urinal when
the landlord joined him. 'Hello. How are you?'

'All right. My lad's outside the gates.'

Clifford looked about the yard. There was no one coming
out to urinate. There were no lights but for those within
the pub. His daughter Mary's bedroom light, which over-
looked the yard, was off and the curtains closed. Clifford
drew back the huge bolt and opened the yard gate a foot
or two.

Standing beside the high, red-brick wall was William.
Behind him were two cases. Ezra said nothing, but
motioned with an incline of his head and William picked
up both cases in his long arms and slipped through the gate.
Both men looked to Clifford. 'Where?' said Ezra. Clifford
walked across the yard and, opening a toolshed door, indicated the place. William placed the cases beside the dusty
bicycle, rusty garden tools and wooden tea chests. He was
not invited to stay and showed no inclination to do so.
Clifford bolted the gate after him, and the two men walked
separately back into the bar.

Ezra took no part in any conversation, but drank in the
corner at his usual table for the rest of the evening. At
closing time he sat on and, when he and Clifford were
finally alone in the bar, Clifford asked him how much he
owed him. The price was half of what Clifford normally

paid for his rum. He flattened the notes on to the bar, poured them both large whiskies, and raised his glass. Ezra met his look, did the same, and their tumblers chinked. Behind the partition the murmur of voices continued.

What had begun as a discreet friendship between Gertrude Benyon, the landlord's wife, and Thomas Beech, the dapper travelling salesman for a surgical supplies firm, had now become little less than an open secret among some of the clientele of the hotel. For all Clifford knew, even Mary, their seven-year-old daughter, had guessed what her mother was up to by now. During the early months of the relationship he had suffered grievously, but gradually he became accustomed to living on the crumbs dropped from the table of his wife's infidelity. He had to. She told him that she would leave him if she could not share herself with this other man. He had to accept it.

Beech he could have killed. At any moment of any minute in any of the day- and night-long hours he could have summoned his small strength and fed it with his giant pain. But only if he were prepared to lose his wife forever. He would not risk it. He did nothing.

Beech and Gertie went out every week. On Wednesday afternoons he would collect her in his Hillman Minx, and they would drive to the Princess Ballroom in Temple Street to the afternoon tea dance. She looked radiant when she left at three. She had the bloom of woman on her when she got back as late as seven in the evening. Clifford raged. He pleaded with her. Begged for discretion, at least discretion, for his sake. For his manhood. 'Tell him not to come and drink here, in my House.'

'But it's not only your House. It's mine, too. If it hadn't been for me, we would never have taken on the place. I made you apply for the tenancy. Without me, we would still be in Aston.'

'I wish to God I'd had the good sense to say no. I should have known what it would be like with you serving men.' There was no conscious irony in his use of the phrase.

Their backgrounds had been very different. He had trained as an accountant, but had never enjoyed the work. His elder brother had gone to university, was something of an academic, and Clifford was a little resentful of him. Edward was a geographer and now taught at a private school in East Anglia. They rarely saw one another. He had never liked Gertie, was himself a confirmed bachelor. He didn't welcome distractions and interruptions in his scholastic life. They had fallen out badly when Clifford had told Edward that he and Gertie were to be married. Until that time, Edward had said little about the attractive woman with whom Clifford was walking out. When the younger man told his brother that they were to be married, Edward told Clifford that he was blinded by her beauty. She was after his small inheritance and he should leave her alone. It stung Clifford to the quick and the brothers had no further communication for some months. And then Edward wrote. They must meet, patch up the foolish quarrel. They were blood.

When they met at the family home in Moseley one weekend soon after, Edward could see that the question of Clifford's marriage to Gertie was not going to be under discussion. He accepted it, but made one plea, as brother to brother, do this one thing: Keep some money aside. Put it aside and don't let anyone know of it. Clifford railed. He knew what his brother was saying and the suggestion that the alluring Gertie was a treasure-hunter was deeply offensive. However, although he could admit it neither to his brother nor himself, somewhere deep in his being, below a level which he was prepared to acknowledge to himself, he harboured a tiny shard of pricking doubt. He didn't want it to be there, and he would not allow himself to think of it. He made the appropriate high-sounding protests about the aspersions that this was casting upon his wife-to-be but, under the gentle, constant and unremitting pressure of his brother, he finally agreed to a piece of foolishness that he said was not worth falling out with that brother for: of the three thousand pounds that their father had left to each of them, he would simply put away half where it would be his and his alone, should he ever need it.

It was in this spirit that, as promised, the very next day, Clifford had pedalled his cycle over to the Midland Bank on Balsall Heath Road and drawn a cheque for one thousand five hundred pounds made out to himself. He then cycled up the Bristol Road until he saw the name of a building society which he knew to be reputable and well-established. He stood outside feeling rather silly, but secretly quite pleased to be doing this furtive thing. At the counter he asked if he might open an account. The manager looked from the young man's cycle clips to the cheque for one-thousand-five-hundred pounds and, not for the first time, wondered what curious story lay behind it.

Edward had insisted that there should be no record of this money and Clifford had experimented with some names as he cycled across Birmingham. They sounded either too prosaic, too John Smith, or else absurdly contrived; he had even begun to hyphenate names and came up with one or two rank absurdities that had made him laugh out loud as he followed a tram up the Bristol Road: Cruddington-Moss; Hawksley-James.

The manager was standing back expectantly now and Clifford's pen was poised; he coughed, turned away and looked at his cycle leaning against the window outside. It was a Rudge. 'Clifford Rudge,' he wrote, and added his brother's address in Ipswich. The manager rolled the pink blotter over the signature and looked at Clifford carefully.

*

Gertie didn't see herself as a treasure-hunter. She had trained as a hairdresser at Whitley's Salon on Ladywood Road. She had swept up and carried magazines and coffee to the ladies under the hair-dryers; then she had washed hair; then shampooed and set. She read all the latest magazines and carefully cut the pictures of the newest styles from them. She had gone to college in the evening to learn how to permanent wave and tint. But she was over-zealous and her so-called friends didn't really like her. They suspected that she was after something, though none of them knew what. She fawned on Joanne Whitley, owner of the salon, and was embarrassing when representatives came to the shop with their wares. She made a great show of being demure and disguised her Birmingham accent. It was rumoured that she was having elocution lessons. Gertie was a sham and the other girls resented it. Her promotion, when it came, was not popular, and they were cruel behind her back. She had feelings. She would have been mortified had she known, but she was living in a world of her own where the reality of others did not easily impinge.

When she was a child of seven she had been playing in the garden when she heard an unfamiliar noise. She ran to the kitchen and found her mother lying there. She went straight to the neighbour's house and Mrs Hooper told Gertie to run to her father at work. He was a silversmith at the Sandpits on Summer Row. She ran the two miles to him on her little frightened shaking legs, wondering all the time if it was even the right way, her eyes filling with tears at each landmark that she recognized that told her that she was on the right course. Her father was amazed to see her, and lifted her up in his arms. When she blurted out the story, he took the corner of his white apron in his hand and tucked it into his bib. And then the two of them ran back along the streets of Birmingham and into the suburb of Ladywood.

Mrs Hooper was kneeling on the floor beside his wife. She was dead at twenty-eight. Gertie was sent next door with the neighbour. Charles took his wife's head in his arms and cradled it in his lap, kneeling on the warm red quarry tiles as the sun lit the tragic scene through the open back door. The bread was half-sliced on the table. The blackcurrant jam beside it unopened.

Before they screwed the coffin down, her father asked Gertie if she wanted to see her mother again. She said yes. As the little girl looked at her young mother without life, Charles asked the child if she wanted to kiss her.

Gertie had new high boots for the funeral of her mother. It was an unseasonably cold day and she was wrapped well against the bitter wind.

From that day on, little Gertie grew more independent as she tried to help her father cope with the grief that he never overcame.

And now, twenty-five years later, that self-sufficiency remained. Arguments with Clifford always ended with the same intractability: I have to be free. Have me as I am, or don't have me at all. The absurd unreasonableness of this position did not occur to her. She had no concept of her husband's feelings. What she had not experienced directly did not exist.

There were only the two of them now on the far side of the partition. Clifford had learned to cope alone, but it was less easy with Ezra at his side. The voices were in whispers, then there were murmurs and laughter. Contained laughter, followed by giggles from Gertie. Clifford squirmed. Ezra felt uncomfortable. He made to leave. Clifford restrained him with his hand lightly on his sleeve. Through the frosted glass it was impossible to avoid the conclusion that the two bodies must be touching, they were so close. 'Can you . . . help?' said Clifford, his voice breaking.

'Help?' said Ezra. 'How?'

'I don't know. That is, I know what has to be done. I don't know how to go on with it. Do you?'

'What do you mean? What are you talking about?'

'I think you know what I mean. You do. Don't make it harder for me, please.'

Ezra had no idea what to say. He knew what Clifford meant, of course. But this was madness. 'Let me think,' he said.

Clifford's white, soft fingers tightened their grip on the other man's big forearm. 'Meet me tomorrow. We can talk. Away from here.'

'I don't know,' blurted Ezra, confused yet mesmerized by these strange words and the warm whisky breath so close to his rough cheek. 'Where? What time?'

'Before we open. Ten o'clock. A little way from here.' The only place that came readily to Clifford's mind was an absurd choice. 'Outside the prison, opposite Winson Green. All right?' Clifford's fingers relaxed their grip slightly.

'All right,' said Ezra. 'Ten o'clock.'

CHAPTER 3

Clifford left the Belle Vue Hotel at twenty minutes to ten. The cleaning woman was downstairs in the bar. Gertie was in bed. He walked down Icknield Port Road, past Summerfield Junior School and into Winson Green Road. Within twenty minutes he was standing across the road from the huge, studded, double doors. He was a few yards from Birmingham's Winson Green prison, waiting to meet a man whom he hardly knew in order to ask him to kill his wife's lover.

The blue July sky and the sun's heat made the purpose of his journey seem even more bizarre. His feet were oozing sweat. Now his forehead was perspiring heavily and he pulled at his sober necktie and then at the stud on his collar. His feet were burning inside his boots. He sat on the low wall, but then immediately got up in case he should be noticed. Did he not want to be noticed because he was going to go ahead with this insanity, he wondered. But he couldn't stop. His loathing was driving him on. He started to walk towards the tram stop down Wellington Street, his feet slippery inside his woollen socks and small black boots.

A breeze picked up somewhere in the dusty street and he stopped and tilted his head up to it. He closed his eyes and milked the breeze into his thin, fair hair.

'Cliff.'

He opened his eyes to the big jaw of Ezra. The man had never used his name before. And no one ever called him Cliff. It was shocking. He wasn't a Cliff, with its suggestion of a relaxed and even, in his mind, a slightly racy man. He was a staid Clifford. But it was curiously appealing too. Was he becoming someone else?

The sweat was trickling into his eyebrows and glistening there.

'Are you all right?' The question registered alarm, not solicitousness. Without answering, Clifford looked up at Ezra and studied his features.

He began a slow involuntary nod of his head. It answered Ezra's question. But he also saw in that face the answer to the question that had not yet been asked.

The two men started down the pavement, away from the prison, the boatman's walk slightly halting as his caliper made its irregular metallic scrape.

Talbot made it easy for him. 'What's his name?'

Clifford could barely say it. It filled his mouth with distaste. 'Beech. Thomas Beech.'

'What's he in?' asked Ezra.

'In?' said Clifford. 'What do you mean, what's he in?'

Patiently, Ezra enunciated: 'What does he do? What's his job?'

Again Clifford looked at the bargeman. Why was he asking these questions? Did he know the questions to ask? Was he even sure what Clifford wanted of him? Would he go to the police as soon as he had been told? No. There was something about him that reassured Clifford that that was out of the question.

'He's a travelling salesman. Chemists. Doctors. Pharmaceuticals. He's a representative. Has his own car. Goes away for two or three days. Then he's back.'

'Too soon, eh?'

'Too soon,' echoed Clifford.

A horse pulling a paraffin cart reared as a car's engine misfired.

'You want him . . . You want me to . . .'

Clifford gathered himself to make the answer to the half-formed question.

'Yes. I want you to get rid of him. It's my wife. She's . . .

Without him my wife and I would be all right again . . .' He said it with hollow conviction. Ezra did not challenge his pathetic faith, even with a look, and said nothing.

The two men turned into Foundry Lane and then around the aptly named open area called Black Patch.

'Why me?' asked Ezra. He needed to allay any suspicions that he had, but in truth he was simply as curious as the question suggested.

'I don't know. I can't do it. I don't know how, or where . . . the body, everything. I'm at my wits' end.'

'So, you came to me. But why me? What do I look like to you?'

'I don't know. I really don't know. You don't look anything. That's part of it. You merge. You're quiet. But I could see you knew what I was going through. I knew you could tell. And I thought you might help . . . have ideas . . . be in a position to . . .'

His voice trailed away as his confidence ebbed in what he was doing, what he was suggesting, and to a virtual stranger. There was a long pause as they sauntered aimlessly on, each man reflecting and considering the next move.

Ezra was intrigued. He was contemptuous of this pathetic man. He wouldn't take from a woman the sort of behaviour that the landlord was taking from his wife. He'd give her a good hiding. It was the way on the cut. But people were different. Especially these fancy types.

'And what do I get? For this "work"?' He drew the word out and sneered at it as he spoke. 'How much?'

'How much? How much should it be? I can pay. I have some money. How much do you think it should be?'

There was a frightening quality in the man's enthusiasm, thought Ezra. He was too earnest. He was probably the greatest danger.

The Bisto kids shuddered by on the side of a rocking tram, sniffing the gravy as they went.

'Five hundred pounds,' said Ezra. 'Two hundred and fifty before, the rest after.'

He had no more idea what to say than Clifford had. But he did know the cost of horse feed and stabling; he knew the price of lugging coal and hauling sacks of cocoa powder. He knew what it cost to shoe a horse and pay a man to walk it. And he knew how every month the work disappeared as every year the tarmac roads spread and the lorries seemed to carry everything that the railways didn't.

'Five hundred,' said Ezra again, confirming his position. And at that moment, as the landlord stood squinting in the sun, his feet oozing sweat, the balance of the luckless travelling salesman's fate was tipped.

Talbot had no idea how he would undertake the murder or how he would dispose of the body. But what he did know without any doubt, was that he was going to do it. About that, he had no reservations. The question of the death penalty, the rope; the thought of a man's blood on his hands, a man whom he did not know, had never met, and who had never harmed him in any way, did not enter into his thinking at all. It was a malevolent deed, and he felt well thinking of it.

Clifford had to get back to the hotel. He would be missed. They must not arouse interest or suspicion. They must certainly not be seen together, except casually, in the Belle Vue. Ezra agreed. They would meet again in about three weeks' time. Even as they parted and Ezra walked away towards the city centre, a plan was forming in his mind. He was enjoying it. He was planning a murder. For the first time that day, probably for the first time that week, a faint smile came to his lips.

CHAPTER 4

A little over three weeks later Ezra returned. August had continued hot, uncomfortably hot. The weather that had been so welcome at first had become oppressive. People sought out the cellar and its cool, the flags of the kitchen away from the range. Dogs became fractious, children irritable, the horses on the street unpredictable. And all the time the pressure grew.

On his route north, Ezra had seen the hay being harvested from the fields that bordered the canal side, and then piled high and wide on the specially constructed outriggers of Staffordshire narrow boats. Now it was all safely stowed in the lofty barns of the surrounding farms. But on this same trip he had also seen crops withering for want of water. He had seen several heavily laden craft run aground, and in the canal-side pubs at Audlem and Market Drayton he had heard of many others. And lying awake at night, unable to sleep for the heat, the beer sweating out of him, he had started to hatch his plan.

He was back in Birmingham. *Crow* was moored at Hockley Brook. It was the third week of the month. The sky darkened through grey and mauve to a worrying green and finally black. At seven o'clock in the evening it was like eleven at night. The first few spats of rain fell. In back gardens the tired beans and wilting potato leaves recoiled under the first big drops. The dust of weeks was beginning to run down the spines of the leaves. The hard paths between the vegetable rows began to splash up their black earth. And then the first great rumbling thunder crashed overhead. In the streets of Hockley, the steep terraced roofs cascaded the water into the gutters, but the gutters could not cope and they spilled over and the down-spouts spewed back.

For over an hour the torrents of rain fell and lightning lit the sky for electric miles. Then, almost imperceptibly, the heavy beating of the rain abated slightly. But it was only a lull and was immediately followed by new and heavier waves.

People cowered within doors, even the drinkers in the pubs stood away from the glass as they looked seriously and silently out of the bar-room windows. And then, quite suddenly, it stopped. This time there was no gradual diminution. The few remaining clouds rolled off to the west and an apocalyptic evening sun burst on the watery scene. Sheds and paths and trees began to steam as the sun warmed them. And then a bird's song. A tentative trill and chirrup, followed by others, and then a door opened here, the sound of a yard brush sweeping away the gathered water there, a man's voice, and a baby crying somewhere.

The storm had cleared the air. The pressure had finally fallen. It was not a time to think of murder. Clifford thought of little else. His greatest hope was that Ezra did so, too.

As Ezra ordered his beer and whisky, the look that was exchanged told Clifford that he need have no doubts; Ezra was still involved.

Clifford had had a dreadful three weeks. Twice he had woken from sleep in terror, bathed in cold sweat, the sheets beneath him sodden. He had a cavity, a little recess beneath his breastbone and, as he lay there, too terrified to move, he could feel the tiny pool of clammy moisture that lay in this shallow lake. Could this woman lying beside him not know his thoughts? Could she lie so close and not feel his loathing, his terror, his excitement?

On each of the three previous Wednesday afternoons she had been out with Beech. He had been in the smoke-room on four nights out of every seven. When he went away, Gertie had a 'headache' and would not come down or, if she did, the smoke-room lacked its usual atmosphere and at closing time the customers were ushered out promptly and with little ceremony.

And, throughout it all, Clifford and Beech maintained a fiction of cordiality, the sort of relationship which might have been expected to exist between landlord and customer.

Beech had moved to Birmingham from Barnsley in Yorkshire, a fact which he did not allow to pass unnoticed. Given that everything—from the cricket played, to the beer drunk, and the houses built—was preferable in Yorkshire, it was not surprising that several of his drinking friends in the smoke-room were heard to ask why he had ever left the place.

These same Birmingham friends were made to feel in some indefinable way culpable for the poor beer, shoddy houses and indifferent cricket of the Midlands. Had it not been for the fact that he bought more than his fair share of rounds of drinks, they might have felt moved to differ with this immigrant's views more forcefully than they in fact did. Instead, they contented themselves with a wry comment when he was out at the Gents, a raised eyebrow between themselves when he was at the bar, and a certain sympathy for the affable landlord who, several of them suspected, was being cuckolded by this self-opinionated and rather irksome man.

Left alone in the bar at closing time, Ezra and Clifford circled one another. Neither knew what the other was feeling, had felt, or planned to do. In truth, each man was experiencing a tremendous subterranean excitement. Clifford hoped that he was on the threshold of destroying his rival, punishing his wife's infidelity and repossessing her. Ezra, while in no way conscious of the reason for his sense of deep thrill, was about to embark on something which would finally allow expression of that latent loathing that he had naturally, since a child, felt for the great mass of his fellow men. As far as his waking mind was concerned, he was simply undertaking something that would lead to the acquisition of a great deal of money, money which he was certainly going to need if and when he left the slow cut, when the cargo, which was getting every year harder to find, finally disappeared completely.

Each also had his doubts. Clifford would not allow himself to think beyond the deed. When he had tried to do so, he had not been able to conjure the image of Gertie as his wife—he, her sole husband. The image became confused and unsure, and he felt unsettled. On this account he no longer tried to predict that area of the future, but concentrated his energies instead on the annihilation of Beech.

Ezra's worries were more specific. Whom could he trust? Where did the dangers lie? How would he do the deed and dispose of the body, and leave no clues or trail which would lead the Birmingham police to him, and himself to the very gallows of Winson Green?

The conversation began in their familiar stilted tones. After each of their meetings, they had to find their relationship again. The time spent apart was too long, or the basis of their 'friendship' too tenuous, to maintain itself during the two- or three-week estrangements. Always the same awkward formality, then the healing power of the friendly liquor, the conspiratorial trust emerging slowly as the two men stood at the bar, hunched together over their tumblers of whisky by the lowered gaslight of the smoky, empty room.

If a breeze were needed to fan the flames of their planned sacrificial bonfire, it blew gently from behind the dark mahogany of the bar partition a few yards away. The

hushed tones, the pauses, and then the laughter. A drink
being poured, the chink of glasses, whispers, more laughter.
The breeze that stirred Clifford's fire of jealousy and loathing blew a gale now. But, for the first time, he was har-
nessing its power and turning it to his advantage.

Gertie's little laugh choked through the partition, and as
Clifford's damp, brown eyes met Ezra's they too betrayed
a little mirth. It gave Ezra the reassurance that he had been
looking for.

A few minutes later the smoke-room door shut and the
gaslight faded through the frosted glass. Gertie walked
briskly through the door which divided the two bars. She
looked at Ezra and he stood up to his full height from his
hunched position at the bar.

'You know Mr Talbot, Gertie? Ezra Talbot, he's been
discussing some business with me.'

Ezra felt exposed and vulnerable as he heard his own
name uttered in this way.

'Mr Talbot,' she acknowledged, looking him carefully up
and down.

'Mrs Benyon,' he said, looking away from her as she
gazed directly at him. Although it was not the first time he
had seen her, it was the first time that he had felt her
presence. She was not like any of the women he had ever
known. She stood her ground. She would be too strong for
Clifford, of that there could be no doubt. If Ezra recognized
this, surely others did. Certainly Thomas Beech had.

For her part she wondered what these two ill-sorted men
were doing. Her husband had few friends. He was adequate
at the bar, serving the customers, chatting about the politics
and sport of the day, but he didn't have a naturally easy
manner. He had no particular friend, and he was often slow
to see a joke or detect a pun. Sometimes she saw that the
regulars had a joke at his expense. He was not what she
called a 'man's man'. He was not easy in a group, particu-

larly an exclusively male group. In this respect he could hardly have been in a less suitable job. However, he was good-natured and well-meaning and it was often said, with all the comprehensive and vague truth of proverbs, that 'he meant no one any harm'.

For Clifford to be at the bar after closing time and sharing a drink with a late customer was not unknown, but it was unusual. To be hunched over the bar with this big man, with his rather grubby clothes and dirty fingernails, his short-cropped hair and pale grey eyes, smacked of something stranger.

She made no attempt to disguise her distaste, and it was only curiosity that led her to look at him again. His head remained still but he gazed at the floor in front of her as she looked up at him.

There was a long and embarrassing silence between the three of them. Clifford did not fill it. Ezra was unable to do so. Gertie experienced feelings unprecedented in her: she felt awkward, superfluous and redundant, feelings which she resented intensely.

It finally fell to her to fill the vacuum. 'Will you lock up, Clifford? I'm going upstairs now.'

'Yes, dear, we'll just finish our drinks and I'll be up too.'

She got to the door that led from behind the bar to their rooms above the pub and turned once more to Ezra. She was not prepared to leave in this manner. She held him for a moment in her gaze, and again he looked away, 'Good night, Mr Talbot.'

'Good night, Mrs Benyon,' he said, not meeting her eyes.

She left the door ajar, and the two men heard her measured footsteps ascend the steep dark stairs and then pad along the landing above them. As she went into the bathroom she could be heard no more.

'Will you do it?' asked Clifford.

It was direct and Ezra found himself slightly shocked.

He said nothing, but tilted his head to the space above them where her footsteps had last been heard and nodded his head twice. Clifford took Ezra's tumbler and filled it with a generous measure. He did the same to his own. As they brought their glasses together each man smiled.

'What does he drink?' asked Ezra. 'What's his tipple?'

'Whisky. Beer. He'll take a rum sometimes. He buys Gertie's port and lemon, of course.'

'That'll do. I've been working it out. I'll tell you as little as you need to know. You're bound to be questioned. The police will know he spent time here. They'll probably uncover his . . .' He paused and inclined his head above. 'With your wife. You'll have to be prepared. You'll be the suspect, the main suspect. It's always the husband if there's been any . . . you know what I mean.'

'I know what you mean.'

'So I'll tell you the least I have to. But you'll have to get him to talk to me. Alone. About getting some drink. Can you do it?'

'Of course,' said Clifford. 'Of course. But Gertie has seen us together. Won't she suspect?' He didn't really want to frame the question for fear of putting any obstacles in the way of the plan.

'What if she does? There'll be no proof. It'll be up to you to act innocent. Anyway, even if they did question me, which I hope they won't, I've got to make sure that there's no clues, no marks, no body to be found. No connection. I'm talking about my life. It's got to be done right.'

Clifford nodded sagely and then added, as if an after-thought, 'It'd be my life too. If they got you, it'd be me too.'

They had drawn closer together across the wide bar and were speaking in hushed tones. Clifford watched Ezra's mouth closely. His teeth were unpleasant. They were strong but yellow, and had a primæval quality about them.

Clifford began to feel the effect of the whisky; his eyes lost focus and he swayed slightly and had to correct his stance by pressing his toes on to the floor through his boots. It would be inappropriate to appear drunk. It might give the impression of carelessness. But the drink also helped. It was easier to talk of these things now. He remembered their daytime meeting of a few weeks ago, near the prison, when they had skirted one another and had had to spit out the words and fill the many awkward gaps in the conversation with surmises.

The door from the stairs, which Gertie had left ajar, suddenly opened and each man jolted erect. Gertie stood there, as before, and looked at Clifford. 'You look as if you've seen a ghost, dear.'

He said nothing. No words would come. Had they been overheard? Surely not. She wouldn't say that. She wouldn't say anything. She wouldn't have entered, even.

'You surprised me, Gertie. What is it?'

'It's Mary. She has a sore throat. She can't sleep. I said she could have a little cordial. I'm too soft with her. Do you have children, Mr Talbot?'

'No, ma'am. I have no children.'

She took the barley water from behind Clifford and said good night, pulling the door to behind her.

'We must take care. I'll go now,' said Ezra. 'I leave tomorrow. In a couple of weeks I'll be back, it depends on the traffic, the locks, the horses, everything. I can't say to a day or two. Get him ready to meet me. That's all you need to do. Tell him I can get him some drink. Tobacco, too, if you like. But not a word to anyone. He mustn't tell anyone else.'

Clifford walked him to the door, pulled back the bolts top and bottom, and let him out into the quiet street. As he walked away, the landlord stood at the door and, rocking very slightly, stared up at the bright August stars that now pierced the clear sky. The smoke that had lingered in the bar for the last half an hour poured out around him. He continued to look above as Ezra's halting step disappeared down the street.

CHAPTER 5

From Birmingham they carried a load of pots and pans to Nantwich, then linen up to Chester, and finally they lugged coal that had come from the Mersey down the picturesque Llangollen arm of the Shropshire Union to Ellesmere.

There were the usual problems: drunks at the locks and wharves, poor stabling, congestion at the infamous bottlenecks, routine disputes among the canal people—company employees and the owner-operators—each keen to load, to get away, to get home, and all to begin the whole business again.

But for the most part things were humdrum: the swaying horse, led by the surly William, ambling from side to hypnotic side down the day-long towpath, Ezra sitting aft and guiding the longboat with the huge S-shaped tiller crooked in his powerful arm.

What William thought of, on this or any other day, no one knew. But Ezra thought of only one thing. He did the deed repeatedly. He made his escape. He posed the questions that might be asked—probably would be asked—and he slipped the noose of each one. He was gone. His tracks were covered in the still, greasy waters of the cut as surely as his boat left no trace of its passing.

In Nantwich, he met his Liverpool acquaintance and bought illicit supplies of rum and whisky and tobacco from the back of a covered Austin wagon on a quiet lane outside the market town. As an afterthought, he asked his supplier if he had any port. Port was duly produced from beneath the grey blankets. Ezra bought half a case. Lately, he was beginning to smile quite frequently.

*

He entered the bar of the Belle Vue Hotel later than usual.
He had spent the early part of the evening with a whore in
Silas Square, his regular sexual outlet when in Birmingham.
She had a small child and it was early, so she laid the child
down in the only bedroom of the terraced cottage and he
thrust himself into her on the carpet square in the middle
of the floor. After the few minutes of pent-up excitement,
which he felt and she feigned, he lay on his back and looked
at her with distaste, her head turned away from him as she
listened for the child next door, her shapeless breasts fallen
back to her armpits, marked blue and red where he had
sucked and finally bitten them violently. His heart thumped
in his chest and a trickle more of semen leaked out of him
on to his thigh.

As he walked slowly through the dusky streets of Handsworth and Lozells towards the Belle Vue, he felt sexually
released, and even his rough being was sensitive to the
evening air. He was savouring the beginning of this dangerous adventure. Soon he would be unable to go back. But
now he was just a free man on an early September evening
walking past urchins at play, women on doorsteps, hawkers
on corners, and public houses with doors open to the late
summer heat.

He and Clifford acknowledged one another with a civil
greeting. Ezra wanted to maintain the rare feeling that he
had garnered on his evening walk. He sat in his corner with
the noise of the bar surrounding him, but it did not pene-
trate his core.

An hour later he walked across the yard to the urinal. A
bedroom lamp was sending a faint glow from an upper
window-pane. With his flaccid member in the fingers of his
right hand, Ezra held himself steady at the urinal with his
left hand in front of him on the wall. By now he was feeling
a little drunk.

There was a belch at his shoulder. It was a sign of male companionableness. He hadn't heard the approach of footsteps. He must be more drunk than he had realized. No, it was his feeling of reverie, his hypnotic state. He was not drunk.

'Ezra?' the voice at his shoulder said.

Ezra could smell the pomade on the man's hair. So this was the smell. The drama was unfolding.

'I'm Ezra. What is it?'

'The landlord, our host, he said you might be able to supply a few of my needs. Some liquor, perhaps some tobacco?'

'I might. Benyon told you, did he?' he asked ingenuously.

'Yes. Wants me to drink myself to death, I should think.'

'Can you keep things to yourself?' said Ezra, folding his member into his rough fustian trousers.

'Always discreet,' said the voice. 'It's my line of work, discretion's called for: medication, people's private matters, private doings. I say nothing. I know how to keep mum.'

'What was it you wanted?' said Ezra.

'I drink whisky. And rum. Can you get me some of each? And Virginia tobacco, some cigarettes perhaps, Player's. As many as you can.'

'Hold on,' Ezra interrupted him, 'hold on. I don't know you. Let's start steady. I sell you too much, how do I know you're not selling it on? The more that know, the more danger there is for me. Let's start steady and see how we go. I'll get you half a case of rum and the other half whisky, and I'll put in some cigarettes, some Player's if I can, then we'll see.'

'That sounds all right,' said Beech. 'When can we meet, and where?'

'Tomorrow. Tomorrow night,' said Ezra.

'That's fine. What time? And where?'

The man was altogether too assertive, too quick, for Ezra. But without pause, he answered, 'At the wharf. Do you know it? The wharf at Nechells, by the Navigation Inn. At nine o'clock. I'll be there, and I'll take you to my supplies.'

'You're a boatman, then?' said Beech.

'Maybe I am, but pay it no mind; the less you know, and the less I know of you, the better. What we're at isn't legal. It ain't a hangin' offence, maybe, but you can't be too careful.'

The men were now facing one another in the gloom, but Beech was unable to see the flicker of a smile that crossed Ezra's lips as he spoke.

'I'll bring some money, naturally, but how much?'

'We'll settle then. You won't be disappointed. To-morrow, at nine. Not a word, no one.'

As Ezra stood in the door ready to leave, Beech gave him a reassuring look, put his finger to his lips and nodded his head from side to side. Of course he wouldn't tell anyone, he knew a good thing when he saw it.

'One thing,' called Ezra in a whisper. 'Do you want a few bottles of good port?'

Beech was about to say no when he thought of Gertie and her liking for port and lemon. Beech was not a cruel man, but this little ploy, which he would share with no one, was too good to miss.

'Bring some if you will,' said Beech.

Ezra nodded an acknowledgement and shuffled off across the yard.

A minute later, as he returned from the Gents, Beech looked up to little Mary's bedroom window. She was sitting there, the curtain drawn very slightly back, the lamp turned low. She was forbidden to play with the other children in the area, but was secretly able to talk to the grown men on their way to the urinal. She liked Beech. He always had a friendly word for her. He knew that her mother did not allow Mary to talk to the passing men, but he took no heed of this and in fact enjoyed the little deception.

'How are you, Mary?' he called to her in hushed tones.

'I'm all right, thank you, Mr Beech. I'm reading, but I'm a bit bored. I'd like someone to play with.'

'I bet you would,' said the avuncular man. He said it with real feeling. It seemed a pitiful life for this seven-year-old, to be hidden away up there, and it made him feel a little annoyed with Gertie. He reached into his trouser pocket and pulled out a sixpence. Placing it on his thumb, he flicked it dexterously up to Mary. It went past her and as it started to fall she reached out her hand and the silver coin dropped into her palm. 'Thank you. Thank you, Mr Beech.'

'Sshh, not a word,' he said, and walked back into the hotel.

As soon as the bar had emptied at closing time, Ezra approached Clifford.

'A drink?' said the landlord.

'Not now,' answered Ezra. 'It's under way. It's best now that I'm not seen around here.' There were calls of 'good night,' from next door in the smoke-room and Gertie's response to her last customers going out through the door.

'I'll be gone now. Say nothing. Do nothing. Act normal. I'll be back in the usual time. Two or three weeks, depending on . . . depending on things.'

'The money,' said Clifford, 'I have the money, the first half.'

'Does anyone know about it?' asked the boatman.

'No. It's money I'd kept separately. For a rainy day.' He bent down beneath the bar and opened his safe. The money was already counted out into a manilla envelope. Ezra took it and shoved it into his trouser pocket. Next door could be heard the familiar little voices of Beech and Gertie. The two men walked to the door and Ezra slipped quietly into the night.

*

The next day the narrow boat *Crow* was unloaded of the pit-props that she had brought down from the Shropshire woodlands, and hauled down the wharf to where the coal was loaded. By early evening she lay low in the water with thirty-five tons of best coal filling her hold. They sheeted her over and, as William shuffled away, Ezra called after him, 'Have the horse ready at four. I want to get away prompt. Real prompt.'

At eight o'clock that evening Beech walked into the smoke-room. He chatted to Gertie at the bar over his whisky and soda, and told her that he had to slip out later for an hour. He should be back before closing time, though. If for any reason he was delayed, he would pick her up tomorrow, Wednesday, as usual. They would go dancing and then back to their usual room at the Midland. He had a little surprise for her. He gave her that lascivious look which reminded them simultaneously of last week's coupling across the broad bed of Room 38 on the second floor. Gertie's blood rose to her neck and flushed up to her face. She asked him where he was going this evening and he gently tapped his nose with the tip of his finger, 'That'd be telling. If you're good, I'll tell you tomorrow. You'll have to be very good, though.'

'Are you sure you want me to be good?' she asked coquettishly. 'Wouldn't you rather I was a little bit bad, a little wicked perhaps?' They laughed, and next door, in the quiet bar, the door open to the warm September evening, Clifford, standing there alone, was able to share the joke.

CHAPTER 6

Ezra was waiting. His hands were damp. He could just hear the faint noise of voices from the Navigation a hundred yards away. He should have said ten, not nine: it would have been darker, with less chance of Beech being noticed. But there were not many comings and goings on the wharf at this time of night. And Beech would be discreet, of this Ezra was sure.

Before he was ready, he heard a footstep on the towpath. What did he mean by ready? He was ready. There was no more to do. How long do you need to wait? Long enough to change your mind? To make off with the landlord's two hundred and fifty pounds and never see him again? What would he be able to do? Tell the police: 'The bloke who was going to kill my wife's fancy man has made off with half of the money'? Nothing. Of course, he could do nothing. But Ezra *was* going to do the deed.

Beech had come early. He had decided to use a taxi. It seemed prudent not to use the car provided by his company for a criminal errand. From the rank at Five Ways the taxi drove down to a spot a couple of hundred yards from the wharf in quiet Cromwell Street. When he had done the deal, he would hail a taxi near the wharf entrance and load his boxes.

Ezra strained to hear the approaching footsteps. They were faltering and hesitant. This was someone who did not know this place.

It wasn't yet ten minutes before nine and he was wandering down the towpath. He passed the *Crow*. Ezra peered out from the crack above the hatch door. The salesman had no idea that it was Ezra's boat. That was good. But it was strange for Ezra to see this man here, in these surroundings, in his suit and shoes, walking slowly, picking his way through the puddles and ruts.

Ezra checked that there was no one in sight in either direction. It was clear. He stepped from the cabin, put a foot on the towpath and called out quietly, 'Oy, mister.'

Beech turned, startled. 'Ezra?' said the voice, surprised but in control. And then again, quietly, 'Ezra.'

'It's me,' said the bargeman. 'Come aboard.'

Beech walked back towards him and stepped on to the fully laden vessel. It rocked very slightly.

'You're early,' said Ezra. 'It's not nine yet.'

Beech had recovered his poise. 'It's the early bird that catches the worm,' he said. 'I've learned that in my business. Be there before the other chap. If you want the business. If you want to make the sale. Get there first. If I say six, I'm there at ten to.'

He spoke in short sentences, and Talbot was not sure when he had finished speaking. At length there was a pause, long enough for Ezra to intervene. 'Yes, you're probably right,' he said. He knew that he wasn't going to be able to deal with this salesman, with his proverbs and quotes and views about everything under the sun. His own boat felt strange to him, filled with this voice, these opinions, these snappy sentences.

They crouched in the cramped, grubby cabin. Beech could not bear even this moment's quiet.

'Right then, have you got some stuff for me?'

'Yes. I'll get it.' Ezra went through the curtain that divided the little space and lifted the straw mattress from on top of the cupboard beneath. He held the lid up with his knee as he brought out a case of drink. He brought it through the curtain and placed it between Beech's open legs. 'All right?' he said.

The man opened the wooden flap and pulled out a bottle

of rum. It was labelled and clean. 'Good,' he said. 'Shall we . . . ?'

Beech wanted to make sure that he was not buying canal water.

'Oh yes,' said Talbot. The salesman's suspicions hadn't occurred to him. He had more pressing concerns.

He reached above the other man and brought down two cups. They were chipped and had the stains of tea rings in them. Beech poured and then turned the cup until he found a small place without a chip. 'Good health,' he said.

He was keen to leave. The atmosphere here was gloomy; not just dirty, but sordid and joyless. No talk, no friendliness. Business didn't have to be like this. Beech was good friends with many of his customers. They had a good time, they shared a joke. 'How much do I owe you? Did you get the cigarettes as well? The port?'

There was a pause. It was too long and Beech felt ill at ease.

'I've got everything for you.'

'I must be getting on, then,' said the salesman. He knew about people. He dealt with them every day of his life. This felt wrong. Bargemen didn't have to be cheerful chaps. All that walking behind dumb horses down narrow cuts probably did make you melancholy, he didn't know. But this felt wrong. It had the awkwardness of courtship. Beech wouldn't have been surprised if Ezra had suddenly made an advance towards him. It was a ridiculous notion, he knew that, but that was the closest he had ever experienced to this feeling. Awkwardness before a sexual deed.

'The other stuff's in there,' said Ezra, pointing through the curtain.

Beech got to his feet and, stooping, put his head through into the tiny space. 'Where . . . ?'

There was no room to swing it fully, but Ezra brought down the iron windlass with all the force that he could muster within the cramped space. Beech must have suspected something, because he had started to turn his face towards his killer. Instead of the back of his head being caved in, the man's terrible fear challenged Ezra for a fraction of a second before his face was made unrecognizable by the first blow. Ezra wished he hadn't seen that half look, that glimpse of terror and—did he imagine it—understanding? He had to make sure Beech was dead, but he wanted more than anything not to remember that look. He stove in the back of Beech's head now that he lay jerking on the floor. The sound was excruciating and as he lifted the angular iron tool each time to bring it down once more, he made a silent scream in himself so that he should not hear the sucking, breaking, bloody bone again.

He was wet and bloody. The man before him on the floor was still and broken. In the great humming silence that followed there was the sound of a plop as a rat slipped into the water from the edge of the towpath. Then, slowly, faintly, the late summer evening sounds of the public house came to him from the distance.

In the canal-side fights that Ezra had so often witnessed, the victor would stand astride the vanquished and wait for any movement that might betray further hostilities. He stood astride Beech. The man was still. The blood now seeped where only a moment ago it had gushed. He had never seen so much blood from a man. He had seen pigs and cattle killed and bled, but this was a man. Had been a man. The sweat of his exertion ran out of his thick, short hair and down his brow. Ezra watched transfixed as a big drop fell right in front of him and splashed into Beech's blood. He shook his head away and reached for a rag. He fell back on to the bunk and wiped his head, all the time watching the seep of the blood as it inched towards his boots.

In the distance there was the sound of raised voices and the smash of glass. A fight? The noise grew as the pub's door must have been opened. More voices. Louder, then quiet, and the general background rumble.

There was a footstep on the towpath. Ezra held his breath and the sweat poured out of him. The voice was talking to itself. It went past. Then it stopped. Ezra couldn't breathe for straining to listen, all the time Beech's blood crawling towards his boots. A man's piss hit the flat waters of the cut and thundered on for what seemed minutes. It lessened. The last drops, and then the boots scraping away up the cinder towpath.

The blood on the floor started to congeal and Ezra began to feel his legs again. He stood, and though he rocked, he didn't fall. He began to wipe, but his actions had none of their usual natural movements about them.

He lowered the bucket quietly over the side and heaved it up in his strong, short arms. The wet rag and then the circular wipe. He started at the top of the cabin, where there were spots and splashes, and worked down the painted timber sides. The dirty water became a rust colour at the first rinse of the rag. The blood had stopped moving, though. It was thick and had the slight skin of congealment upon it.

There was no point in doing any more now. He had to deal with the body. There was more noise from up the towpath at the Navigation. Then it fell away. They were walking in the opposite direction towards the road. He laid the hessian sacks, collected easily, indistinguishable one from another, and used by many poor boat people as bedding, on the floor of the cabin. He then pulled at the body of Beech. The head rocked plaintively and the limbs flailed. When he was on the sacking, Ezra strung him around the neck and waist and ankles. He was a neat parcel of a man now and Ezra looked down at his tidy work with satisfaction. The sack was wet at the head again, the wounds seeping from the movement of the body. Ezra pushed some rags towards the blood and reached his cup of rum to his lips.

The heavy sheets that covered the hold were big and awkward. He manœuvred the stern one a few feet back and started to fill a pail with the biggest coals that he could find.

He quietly lowered the pail of coal into the water and then, with a hand beneath the bucket, he tipped out the contents and spilt them through the water to the bottom of the cut. He lowered every second bucket from a different place over the side of the boat. A dozen pailfuls and he had scooped a shallow in the coal-hold sufficient to contain a man. He replaced the hold sheets and went back into the cabin. There was a hint of rain and thunder in the air.

He eyed the walls and ceiling of the cabin with satisfaction. The only untoward thing was the shape lying bound in its hessian rags on the deck between the bunks.

He picked up the cup of rum that Beech had begun to drink from an hour ago and sat in his customary place in the corner of the bunk. He stretched out his legs, but there was no place for them on the floor. With macabre irreverence, he crossed his boots and lowered them on to the bundle in front of him. They sank comfortably into the soft underbelly of Beech's corpse. Within ten minutes Ezra was asleep, the dark rum cradled in his hand.

CHAPTER 7

Gertie was surprised that Tom did not return. It wasn't like him. He had said he might be delayed, but he was a salesman and he always made alternative arrangements. She felt mildly annoyed with him, as if it were a slight to her. He had been a little cavalier with her lately. She could hardly say that he had begun to take advantage of her, but he had become just a touch dismissive where once he had been attentive. The presents still came. The avowals of love, affection, and yes, sometimes, lust. But had she been right to detect a certain waning of the early enthusiasm? He was close to sleep before he had finally roused himself to make love to her last week at the Midland. They'd had a late lunch and he had drunk too much, and they'd had a dance or two in the afternoon and then come up to their room, and he had actually closed his eyes for sleep while she got ready—was quite startled to be woken. But when he had come to, he was good, she remembered, very uninhibited, and she had been rather ashamed when they looked at one another later and the look referred to what they had done. But he had slept, or been ready to, before wanting to make love. And now, this evening, he hadn't come back.

She looked up at the sound of every hand upon the door but read the shapes as not being his before they materialized through the thick frosted glass of the Mitchells and Butler's door. When he could no longer come, she called time two or three minutes early and the regulars looked at her, and one another and, surreptitiously, at watches slipped from waistcoat pockets.

*

Clifford was in a state of high excitement. Would Beech return, or was this unbelievable event really happening? Could he be involved in the murder of a man? Surely it was a dream. It wasn't a nightmare. He wasn't frightened, just unbelieving. Talbot would walk in and say that it couldn't be done. Clifford would peer into the smoke-room and see Beech at his usual place at the bar or on a stool just around the corner from the partition.

But it wasn't so. There was no tinkling laughter from behind the glass and mahogany. His wife was silent. He could sense the proximity of her presence. It was oppressive. She showed her feelings, always had, couldn't help it. When they had been younger, and closer, they had joked about it. Hurt, tears would prick her eyes; angry, she would scratch or shout. He could feel her anger and disappointment now. From a few yards away, he could sense her.

From the bar he heard her call, 'Time, gentlemen, please,' and looked at the clock.

The regulars wouldn't approve. No one likes early calling of time. One of his customers caught his eye and glanced at the clock above the bar. Clifford shook his head. The gesture said to ignore the call from next door, to relax and drink in your own time.

He began to believe that Talbot really might have done the thing. Perhaps Beech would not be at the rear of the pub at two o'clock tomorrow afternoon to collect Gertie for their 'drive'. Perhaps his torment was over. He felt elated. He put a tumbler to the inverted whisky bottle and glugged in a double measure. As he put it to his lips and tipped his head slowly back, he became aware of Gertie watching him from the space between the two bars. He continued to drink and she to look at him.

Ezra was woken by a rhythmic pattering on the boat. He started up and tried to take in everything around him. A body at his feet. A dark bloody stain at the head. A cup on the floor and the smell of the sticky rum beside it. A beating of heavy rain on the roof of the boat, and the curtain thrash of it on the cut. As he pushed open the cabin door there was a crack of thunder not far away and, almost immediately afterwards, a fork of lightning. It was a good sign, he thought. The world was black. Everyone, even thieves and prying eyes, would be under cover in this weather. He staggered towards the stern hold sheet and drew it back a yard.

Even for this strong man the body was awkward in its lifelessness. It flopped and collapsed in the confined area. In the rudder space he stumbled, and Beech's body fell across the hatches and slipped to the wet floor. He gathered him up again and this time, the body slung firmly on his shoulder, he made his way gingerly down the side of the boat until he got to the open hold. The rain was pouring down his neck and shirt and soaking his trousers. He threw the bundle of body on to the hold cover and then rolled it down into the space that he had made for it. He jolted its legs up and down and moved a few coals from behind where the head lay. It was a good fit. He was pleased. He threw back his head to cast the rain out of his hair and face.

A few minutes later and he was back with pieces of old sacking. These he filled with several large coals each and tied them at their necks. He worked in blackness and the roaring rain. But every few minutes he stood electrified as the lightning that followed the great claps of thunder exposed him brilliantly. When he had filled four of his little 'sacks' with coal, he put them back around the body, pulled down the sheet and lashed it tight. The rain poured on to him, the thunder began to rumble further away, and the lightning lit up someone else's deeds, not his.

He washed his hands over the side of the boat and stepped below into the cabin. As he took off his shirt and boots and soaking trousers, the steam of him rose and gave off a good smell. He dried himself roughly and crawled under his blankets. Just as he was drifting into sleep he sat up and, in the darkness, put his hand into the space on the floor between the bunks. He flapped it around, up and down and across.

CHAPTER 8

A day out on the canal, a ride on a barge, was just one of
the treats that the enterprising minister of the Marston
Methodist church and Sunday school had organized since
his arrival at the parish less than a year ago. His populist
policy seemed to be working. The congregation had gradually swelled. The neighbouring Anglican vicar only stiffly
acknowledged his rival on the street these days. There had
been many defections across the village to the unprepossessing grey building that, in spite of its drab exterior, swayed
to evangelical affirmation, twice on Sunday and once of a
Wednesday evening.

Some of the children cared less for the teachings of Wes-
ley and Whitefield and the hymns of brother Charles than
they did for the popular Sunday outings. Some of the adults
too, if the truth were told.

When William Pemberton had retired as a haulier boatman in 1929, rather than sell his boat for next to nothing,
he had painted the craft in yellow and blue (rather badly)
and fitted slatted benches and a canopy like those on the
lakeside steamers that he had seen on postcards. Nowadays,
on pleasant Sundays, and by arrangement, he took parties
up and down the canal. It was pleasant work and the
crowds loved it.

At eleven-thirty, directly after church and a sermon that
had been heeded even less than usual, the congregation,
and one or two who had not even attended the church,
made their way through the little Shropshire village and
down to the towpath at Little Onn bridge.

Mr Smythe was beaming. He marched at the front, his
flock trailing in his wake. Down the steep High Street, and

past the tobacconist's with its yellow Cellophane sunshield which made the goods look remote and unattractive. Past Mrs Hallett's milliner's shop with the few hats displayed in what was no more than her front parlour window. Down past Jones and Son the ironmongers, and the Grapes on the corner, with the smell of last night's tobacco and beer hanging faintly in the still, Sunday morning air. The children were in a state of high excitement and skipped along in groups of two or three, best friends and second-best friends, all friends today. A day on the canal. For some, the first time that they had ever been on it.

Daisy held hands with Louise and Louise held hands with Victoria and Victoria pretended not to notice the proximity of Albert who jostled Trevor to try and win the attention of Victoria. Their parents were more staid but nearly as excited. No roast to cook, but a mound of fresh sandwiches to eat, and cake to follow—no custard to make today. A bottle of ale for father and mineral waters and cordial for the children and tea in a flask for the ladies. The sun was shining; there was talk of yesterday's football results, the weather, the crops to be brought in and those safely gathered, and how far they would go towards Gnosall.

At the bridge there was much excitement as the children saw the cut, even though most of them had seen it many times before. Two hundred yards down the towpath, unhitched and making its stately swaying progress towards them, was the great grey Shire that was going to tow them up and back down the canal.

Mr Smythe took out his list of names. There were calls for quiet as he checked that all were present. He had done this not thirty minutes ago outside the church. The likelihood that anyone should have got lost between there and here was remote indeed, but he seemed to enjoy his self-imposed task. People called names present for those that could not hear and those that they could not see. Many were called twice. After ten minutes of this increasingly futile and frustrating performance, the long-suffering minister gave up and folded the paper away in his inside pocket.

As the horse munched from its leather bucket and swished a lazy tail at the noonday flies, the boatman ushered everyone aboard, helping the ladies up the step that he had thoughtfully provided, advising the children to remain seated once on board for fear of the water. The horse littered the towpath and Sidney lamented his wife's prevailing on him not to bring a bucket to collect the droppings for his roses. The neat little piles steamed and then cooled as the barge lowered into the water under the throng.

At last, and none too soon for the children, the owner gave the call to his lad and the horse was stirred into action. A great cheer went up as the slack of the rope was drawn out and the boat was slowly tugged away. Gradually, the steady, ambling rhythm of the horse's gait metamorphosed down the rope into a measured glide through the still waters.

The boat's movement had a hypnotic effect on everyone, and after the initial shouts and cheers and excitement, a calm and near-quiet descended. Soon, they lost sight of their bridge and road, and in half an hour they could see only the spire of the church at the top of the town. A gentle curve later and their town was no more. Some of the youngsters had never been this far from their homes before, and they moved quietly closer to the big skirts of their mothers or the bare arms of their fathers. The boatman had seen it all before. The excitement, the crush as if they wouldn't all get aboard; the jostling for places, the departure, and then the quiet that settled on the crowd soon after.

The minister made his way to the stern and spoke to the boatman. He then walked to the front of the craft and, standing in the prow, with just a passing thought of Jesus preaching from the boat on the sea of Galilee, he asked for

quiet (it already was) and told his flock that they would be
going as far as Cowley Tunnel, just this side of Gnosall,
about two hours away, and that there they would lunch
while the rudder was attached at the other end of the craft
and the horse was rested before towing them back.

Just as they had been glad to get on the boat two hours
ago and couldn't wait for it to leave, so, as the time passed
and the craft went through ever new and unfamiliar surroundings, the children couldn't wait for it to stop, so that
they might play on the towpath, which had never looked
so interesting and full of exciting possibilities as when it
was travelling by them at a regal two miles per hour.

With Cowley Tunnel in sight a hundred yards away, the
converted narrow boat bumped gently into the side and the
boatman slipped a loop around one of the several mooring
spikes that were driven in here for boats to await their turn
in passing through the short tunnel.

The small crowd spread out. The children played, the
women prepared the food from baskets and found the best
spots in the fields and hedgerow. Some of the men immediately began to walk towards the bridge over the opening
to the tunnel in the certain knowledge that not far down
the lane they would find the Hare and Hounds pub, for
although they had been on the canal for nearly two hours,
they were no more than five miles from their own village.

As the haulier sat in the stern of his empty craft and ate
his bread and cold pork chop and drank his sweet cold tea,
his lad led the horse over the bridge and tied him in the
shade so that he might rest and feed for an hour or two
before the slow pull back up the cut.

Susannah caught a glimpse of something bright on the path.
The sun struck back from it and she moved her head
instinctively and then had to shift it again to track down
the object. She moved to it and picked it up. It was a little

gold button. No one had seen her and, although she was a good little girl, her first thought was to keep her treasure for herself and tell no one of her find. Her second thought was more in her nature: she needed to share the knowledge of her find with her friends. She called Louise and held the little button between her thumb and finger. Louise wanted to hold it, but Susannah refused. The boys arrived to see what was being examined.

'It's got something on it,' said George, grabbing the button and causing Susannah to wail. This had no effect on George, who turned his back on her and examined at arm's length the scrolling on the button.

'It's some letters,' he told William, who stood at his shoulder.

'They're all mixed up, I can't read them.' George's reading ability, even when confronted with 'big letters' on a blackboard was not of the best. Susannah's crying had attracted her mother's notice and she unceremoniously retrieved her daughter's prize, at the same time giving George a sound slap on the head. She immediately thought that the little object was gold and probably valuable, and she regretted the attention that had been paid to the find. It was somehow in the public domain now, whereas had nothing been said it might well have been sold at a profit to a jeweller in Wolverhampton. Perhaps there would be a reward if it were to be returned to its rightful owner? But who dropped gold (if it was gold) on a canal towpath, and could anyone so careless be found?

'What is it?' said the solicitous voice beside her. The question didn't relate to the object in her hand, but to the general commotion that surrounded the scene. Susannah had stopped crying, but George, either feeling hard done by or seeking some sort of protection from further attack or accusation, had decided to adopt similar behaviour. He was a big, grubby, sweaty child and no one sought either to comfort him or to ascertain the reason for his intermittent wailing, but he frequently peeped through his hot, dirty hands to see if his performance was having any effect.

Misunderstanding his question, Susannah's mother proffered the button to the minister. Mr Smythe examined it. 'It's a cuff-link. It's the front half of a cuff-link with the owner's initials in scroll. It must be gold and is probably sorely missed. I'm sure the owner will be immensely relieved to have it returned. I wonder how it was that it was lost down here. Not many folk on barges wear gold cuff-links I wouldn't have thought, would you, Mrs Pryce?'

'No, Mr Smythe,' she replied rather dispiritedly as she saw him slip the link into his waistcoat pocket and give it a reassuring little pat.

'I'll make sure it's taken in to the police station as soon as I'm in town tomorrow.'

'I could take it,' said Susannah's mother, but with little conviction or hope of success.

'It's quite all right, Mrs Pryce. It'll be my pleasure. I have to go into Newport first thing tomorrow morning in any event. I'll make the police station my first call.'

As a last resort, a rather feeble plea came from the thwarted lady. 'Do you think that there might be a reward, Mr Smythe?'

'I think that the owner might be so pleased to have his property returned that he might show some gratitude, particularly if the item were of sentimental value, bought by his wife perhaps. But in any event, as I am sure you know, ma'am, your reward for all good and honest deeds lies not in this place or at this time, but in a better place, and at a future time.'

'Yes, of course,' said Mrs Pryce, without perhaps the enthusiasm that the preacher might have wished to hear in her voice.

The children had recovered from both the excitement of

the find and the ensuing travail and upset which it had
caused, and were now all playing together as if they had
never seen a gold cuff-link lying in the cinders of the
towpath.

At nine-thirty the next morning, the churchman was giving
the desk sergeant at Newport Police Station full details of
the place and time of the find and of the finder's name and
address—'Should there be any wish, on the owner's part,
to contact the good woman, a woman, if I may say so,
Sergeant, of good character but limited means, to whom a
few shillings would no doubt be most welcome.'

The sergeant examined the cuff-link and then laid it carefully beside the lost property book on the broad, dark-oak
counter. 'One moment, please, sir,' he said to the minister.
He returned with a large magnifying glass and, taking
advantage of the best light, he held the link above him and
scrutinized both sides with the glass. 'Uuum, nine carat
gold,' he pronounced, and then, turning it deftly in his big
fingers with their rather dirty nails: 'It looks like . . . T.L.B.
Difficult to tell with that scroll engraving, but that's what
it looks like to me.'

'May I look, Sergeant?' said Mr Smythe, who was
intrigued and, as he felt, not entirely disinterested in the
proceedings.

The sergeant passed the magnifier and the link to Mr
Smythe who breathed on the link, rubbed it on his worsted
sleeve, then played the glass to and fro. 'I think it's T.*H*.B,
Sergeant.' Then, showing some humility, 'The scrollwork
does make it exceedingly difficult, but I think those curls
at the top are the top of the "H". Have another look.'

He agreed. It was T.H.B. 'We'll make inquiries, sir. See
if anyone's reported it lost. Have a look at the papers, in
the Lost and Found. It'll no doubt find its way back to its
rightful owner, things usually do, you know.'

'Thank you, Sergeant. Good luck and God be with you.'
The sergeant touched his forehead in embarrassed acknowledgement of this salutation. It was not Sunday and this was
not church. These Methodists were a bit too direct. He
could see why they got under people's skin.

'Good day, sir. We'll do our best and I'll be in touch if
we have any success.'

The sergeant dropped the link into a little brown envelope, tied a label through the hole punched in it specially
for the purpose, and put it in the green metal cabinet in the
back room where the smaller items of lost property were
held.

He thought how unlikely it was that anyone would claim
the item. He'd been in the police force for over twenty years.
Bargemen and their employees didn't wear nine-carat gold
cuff-links. But even the best-dressed men needed to take
their Saturday-night women somewhere for their sport, and
the canal bank was always a quiet place where you were
guaranteed a good flat path to a quiet field. You could hear
anyone coming, too. The sergeant knew in his own mind
that someone a bit better than he should be had been down
on the canal towpath with someone no better than she
should be. The man had gone home a pound or two lighter,
the woman had the money, and the cuff-link was on the
third shelf of the green metal cabinet and there, he felt sure,
it would stay.

The woman who found it should have kept it, he thought.
She'd have made a few pounds from the nearest jeweller. I
wonder why she didn't? Probably something to do with that
preacher.

T.H.B., he thought, as he put the kettle on. Must be
someone local, if not local, not very far away. The initials
did sort of ring a bell, yet he couldn't just place them.

CHAPTER 9

'Daddy, what's the matter with Mother?' The question was uncharacteristically direct. Clifford and his daughter were supposed to be shopping, though neither of them had picked up the hastily written list. It was still lying on the kitchen table. What they had needed was not shopping but to get out.

It was Saturday afternoon and the pub had been closed for an hour. Clifford had had a sandwich, Mary had been in her room, and Gertie was nowhere to be seen.

In recent days much of the communication between the married couple had taken place through the door of what had become her room. She had not served in the smoke-room since two days after the disappearance of Beech. She hadn't eaten a meal with the family, nor gone to the shops, or walked through the hotel.

When Clifford had glimpsed her on the dark landing, she looked thin and drawn, without make-up and not properly dressed. When he had stood in front of her and tried to talk to her, she had looked through him. She didn't want the doctor, she said. No, she didn't want to eat just at the moment. She would be all right. She needed to be left alone for a little while. That's all she would say. Clifford concurred.

'She's not very well, a bad dose of 'flu,' he told the staff and the regulars. By the end of the first week he had hired a new barman. The hotel was running as well as ever. But upstairs, little Mary was worried. Her mother, always distant and remote, a woman who lacked natural maternal affection, had now become a pale spectre that the little girl passed silently on the dark landing.

Now, as they walked among the Saturday afternoon shoppers, her father took the little girl's hand in his and tried to reply. 'I think you're old enough to know,' he said awkwardly. 'Your mother is having what we call ladies' problems. At a certain age, ladies go through changes in their bodies that make them feel a little bit odd.' This was patently absurd. Clifford knew as little about menopausal change as any other man living in Icknield Port Road in 1933, but he did know that it was not something that was likely to affect his thirty-three-year-old wife for some years yet. However, the mysterious and sexual connotation struck him as being fitting in some way, and the vague nature of the malaise suited his purposes in trying to explain away his wife's strange symptoms and behaviour to their curious daughter.

'How—"odd", Daddy?' pressed Mary, immediately intrigued by this information and frankly surprised that she had not simply been fobbed off with a gentle but final, 'It's nothing to do with you, everything's going to be all right.'

'It's to do with growing up and being a woman and then—' he struggled for words to make sense to himself, let alone Mary—'and then growing . . . down again . . .'

'Growing down? What does that mean, Daddy? Getting smaller again, like old people do?'

'Well, that's the sort of idea. It's difficult to explain. Especially for men. When you're a bit older I'll, or Mother'll, explain it all to you.'

'Is she going to be all right?' asked Mary, in a tone of factual inquiry rather than affection.

'Of course she is,' came her father's hasty and unconsidered reply. 'She'll be fine in a week or two. We should just try and be quiet around the house and let her rest. Now, where's the list?'

Mary was only seven, but she knew the difference between a change of subject and a genuine question, and consequently she didn't respond but continued to wonder when, if ever, she would begin to understand her parents, the things they said, and the way in which they behaved to one another.

When Beech had not returned on the Tuesday evening, Gertie felt discomfited. When he didn't call for her in his little car for their Wednesday afternoon liaison, she felt absurd. It was one thing to be dressed and leaving at two-thirty, floating past her tormented husband and giving him nothing to hold on to but the scent that filled the air as she wafted by, but it was quite another to be sitting and waiting in the upstairs parlour, swatting her cream soft kid-leather gloves into the palm of her hand and walking to the window to peer down the main road every two or three minutes.

Tom was never late. Something was wrong. How could he do this to her? The embarrassment, the indignity; she would never forgive him this behaviour. He knew how awkward it was for her to get out of the house without a fuss. She had explained to him the arguments that she had to endure every week on her return. The accusations, the recriminations, the threats. And yet she was prepared to go through all this for him. No longer, she thought. I shan't do it again. This is the end. But still she sat there, only dimly aware of how far her growing anger and frustration indicated her involvement with her lover.

By ten to three it was obvious that he was not coming. Clifford was stocking the bar downstairs. In a barely controlled rage she swept towards the door. She was too embarrassed to meet Clifford's look, but was equally unable to resist it. And she quizzed that fleeting look. What did his glance mean as she flew out of the door? What was newly missing? It was the hurt; that was what had gone.

Slightly but crucially over-dressed for walking down the busy afternoon street, Gertrude hurried along towards

Beech's lodgings in Gillott Road. She had never been there, but she knew where the road was. She had no idea what she was going to do when she got there; she certainly couldn't knock at the door and ask his landlady if he was in. But she needed to get out of the Belle Vue, and that she had done.

Was she imagining it, or were people looking at her and sniggering? She walked more quickly and was aware that her face was flushed and her eyes were filling. It was the dust of the afternoon street, she told herself, and made her feet march steadily, one before the other in a measured pace, in an attempt to find her composure.

She turned off the main road down into Carlton Hill. It was quieter, more suburban, and she slowed down and told herself that she was being absurd to become so worked up about one missed appointment.

But it was no good. In spite of herself she had begun to walk more quickly again and, out of the dust now, her eyes were still full and ready to burst. She rounded the corner into Gillott Road and instinctively looked behind her. There was nothing to be seen. Nothing out of the ordinary. The bread man was delivering down the leafy road.

It was No. 53. She didn't need to go there. She could see in the nearly empty road the little fawn Hillman Minx. The car was parked outside his lodgings. He was there. He must be. But why? Was he ill? So ill that he couldn't send a message? And so suddenly? It made no sense. She walked down the road, past the lime trees with their sticky summer leaves, looking first this way, at the car ahead of her, and then that, up to the house. She didn't know which was his room but he had told her that it was at the front of the house. As she drew level she stopped and looked up, but there was nothing that would indicate anything amiss. All the curtains were drawn back, the top window in each room was open a little, the net curtains behind them moving slightly in the breeze.

After his tea the police sergeant walked up to his allotment. Sometimes, when he was on two in the afternoon until ten in the evening, he would walk up to what he called 'my other patch' to have a look at his fruit and vegetables by early moonlight in the autumn or in the late dusk of summer. And when he was on ten at night until six in the morning he would certainly spend a little of that early daybreak time in the vicinity of his plot. There was not so much crime in Newport that a man couldn't arrange to be near his sprouts and runner beans once or twice a day, felt the even-tempered sergeant.

His garden put him into a special frame of mind. He preferred being there alone. He had never directly declined his wife's occasional offers to come up to the plot and see how things were growing, but in truth he was relieved when she asked him to bring back a marrow or some freshly dug potatoes, rather than offering to come with him.

Many of the men up on the allotments were of the same ilk. They greeted one another, exchanged the time of day, would share their muck with you in autumn and even reluctantly praise your good onions in August, but, civilities over, they seemed to prefer their activities to be solitary, even somnambulistic. They built up a quiet rhythm at the task in hand, sowing or digging or hoeing, and, if the sergeant was anything to go by, fell into a pleasant reverie from which they did not welcome disturbance.

It was the third week of September, a fine evening, and the sergeant smelt the very first hint of autumn. There was that delightful little snap in the air and a clarity in the way the smoke from the chimneys hung there.

He unbolted his toolshed and got down the big hoe. It

had a long thick handle which he had only fitted this year. It made hoeing a greater pleasure than ever. There was little effort required and the blade churned through the dark soil with ease. Of all gardening jobs this was his favourite: treading between the rows, working the hoe in and out as he went, a step back each time, building up the steady rhythm that allowed you to come just so close to the tender roots of the beans and peas, the balls of beetroot and plunging parsnips.

The light was fading, and Jack Dillon's little fire of garden debris at the far end of the plots glowed as the breeze found out its heart. This was the best time at the best place in the best season, thought the sergeant. There was nowhere that he would rather be. The football pools' winners in the pages of the *News of the World* had no better luck than he. He wouldn't change this moment for all their money.

Perhaps it was this half-recollection, the idea of people's faces, faces in the newspaper, hazy prints made up of thousands of dots, that brought the image to his mind, but suddenly, unbeckoned, it was there. Immediately, he put the hoe back in the shed and bolted the door. No gardener leaves hoeing in the middle of a row, and certainly not the sergeant.

'What can we do for you, Sarge?' said the desk officer. The sergeant ignored him and walked up to the missing person posters that hung on the wall behind the desk. '*Thomas Henry Beech, last seen in the vicinity of the Belle Vue Hotel, Ladywood, Birmingham, on the evening of Tuesday, 5th September 1933. If you have any information concerning the whereabouts of the above person, please contact your local police station immediately.*'

The sergeant knew that it was unnecessary but, even so, he opened the metal cabinet in the back room and undid the string on the brown envelope. The link slipped into his hand. The desk officer watched his performance closely.

With a nod of his head in the direction of the poster behind him, the sergeant dropped the link into the younger man's hand. 'Get CID on the 'phone,' he said, 'Birmingham, Steelhouse Lane.'

CHAPTER 10

The dredging itself was a desultory affair. On the basis of such scant evidence, the detective-inspector from CID had been frankly sceptical about the likelihood of finding a missing person from the Birmingham area in a canal near somewhere called Gnosall, outside Newport, Shropshire.

And so it was left to the local police to carry out the search. They lacked any specialized equipment and simply walked down to the canal-side, just before the entrance to Cowley Tunnel. The gardening sergeant and his two constables, in their waders and gumboots, stood at the edge and looked at one another to see who was going to show initiative in this uncharted territory.

A couple of boys leaned over the bridge a hundred yards away, but the policeman stationed there prevented their walking down the towpath to satisfy more fully their curiosity. Barges and narrow boats passed this spot, as many as three or four an hour, sometimes in 'trains' of two or three together and, like embarrassed children, when a barge hove into view the policemen ceased their preparations and stood idly by, acknowledging the passing craft with a serious nod of the head.

At ten-thirty, immediately after a diesel-powered narrow boat and its butty had disappeared into the tunnel, the sergeant took the initiative.

Little Susannah had shown him the exact spot where she had found the link. It was just by this mooring spike, she had said. The sergeant cast the grappling iron into the slightly moving waters and carefully trawled it back to him. It bumped and rocked on the puddled bottom. When it was level with him he hauled it out, gathering the rope neatly into big wet loops as he did so. He slung the hook a little wider this time, reaching the centre of the canal and the deepest part. The iron was drawn down and across to him. He cast again. The crowd of idlers on the bridge had grown. There were at least eight or ten of them and they sensed the excitement of the search.

This time, just as the hook came towards him, it caught something, before immediately losing it again. He cast to the same place and hauled in. Within a few feet he had hold of something. Something was rocking and turning his hook and rope. He steadily and gently hauled the catch to the side of the towpath beneath him. The two constables had drawn closer. They all leaned over but could see only a dark, indistinct shape moving to the tug of the hook. They each took a portion of the rope and began to haul. The load fell away, and to cries of delight from the bridge, all three men stumbled into the hedgerow behind them. The normally placid sergeant shouted to the policeman at the bridge to move the crowd. 'Get them off there, shift 'em off home,' he called. He didn't wait to see the result of his plea but dropped the iron hook in where it had just broken free, felt it catch the load as he took the strain, and handed it to the constable. He then dropped another one in four or five feet further down and tried to do the same. The first time it slipped by, finding no purchase. At the second attempt though, it caught. He gave them the signal to gently draw out the load.

It could be nothing but a body. As it broke the surface in its hessian bag, an arm flapped out, the hand white and green and withered away. The great weight of the body was on account of the rocks which had been tied head and foot to hold the body down. But that same weight must have caused the sacking to tear, or perhaps it had caught on the hook because, like a guilty secret, the man's arm was poking out obscenely, as if summoning help.

*

Shortly, there was less to see as the body was hastily covered with a sheet. But the bridge was now crowded with the townspeople who flocked to the scene. There was high excitement. Sergeant Ennals had found a body. Sergeant Ennals, who did a garden next to this one, lived near that one's sister, drank in the pub, played football until last year for the police team against the miners and the local pub sides; Sergeant Ennals, whom everybody knew and who was the most ordinary chap in the world, had just pulled out of the canal a dead body. This was better than three Christmases.

At two feet, as opposed to a hundred yards, the feelings were different. This was someone, not just a body. There were bits of fingers and a ring on one of them. There were boots laced and knotted, double bows. There were hollows where once there were eyes. This was someone who was no longer anyone. The older constable, a man in his mid-twenties, had been sick as soon as the corpse had flopped up over the edge of the canal. Now the other one was retching into the early fruits of the tangled blackberries at the bank. The sergeant held his nostrils against the wretched stink and moved upwind. A barge came into view. As it approached it slowed, but the sergeant gave a curt command to keep going. The bargeman reluctantly did so, but the rest of those on board came to the side of the craft and peered silently at the shape beneath the sheet.

CHAPTER 11

Once, when the Inspector's wife and daughter had gone to visit her parents in Mid-Wales, he had brought some sweet-william into the house from the back garden. It made a pretty sight on the table; he had grown it himself and it reminded him of his absent wife. (Though, to tell the truth, while he loved her dearly, and little Emily was the apple of his eye, it was very nice to have peace and quiet in the house, to make a meal with the back door open and enjoy it with a bottle of ale and the evening paper, instead of sitting at the dining table and listening to the day's events.)

Two days after they had gone (he saw them off on the train from Snow Hill station to Newtown) there was a big robbery in the jewellery quarter in Hockley and the Inspector was suddenly working sixteen and seventeen hours a day. So much for peace, quiet and the evening paper. Two of the gang were caught quickly, they were small fry and had tried to 'fence' some identifiable goods in Coventry within a week of the robbery. Thank goodness for amateurs, thought the Inspector, without them police work would be that much more difficult. Amateurs, a lot of greed and very little patience, were great aids in the detection of crime, he had always found. The rest of the gang proved more difficult to locate, and even when all five of them were eventually in custody, more than half of the stolen goods remained 'unaccounted for'.

The day before his wife and Emily were due back in Birmingham, the Inspector made a methodical tour of the blessedly quiet house. He could hear the clock ticking in the hall while he was on the first landing. All was well.

Perhaps the banister needed some polish, but the house was clean and tidy.

He opened the door to the front parlour. The afternoon sunlight was pouring into the room. It split the dark red chenille tablecloth in half. The sweet-william were over. The pink blossoms had faded, the red had started to shrivel and the white had begun to go an unpleasant shade of brown around their frayed edges. He took the vase and carried it carefully to the brown enamelled sink in the scullery at the back of the house and pulled out the dead flowers. The smell of putrefying vegetable matter made him retch.

Compared with the dreadful smell of the decayed and decomposing body that lay before him on the canal towpath now, the smell of the rotting flowers had been a summer fragrance. He put his handkerchief to his mouth and nostrils and looked at the corpse with his head inclined. The two constables exchanged a self-satisfied glance. The Inspector from Birmingham CID felt as distressed now as they had themselves a couple of hours ago. It was their first murder and by now they had begun to feel a little possessive and rather proud of their corpse.

The news of the finding of the body in the water reached Talbot almost as quickly as if it had come by train. He was moored at Hargrave outside Tarporley, far up into Cheshire on the Shropshire Union. It had been his wish to make a long run, to get as far away from the Midlands as was possible for a while. He had been beyond Chester, but now he was on his way back, carrying bales of cotton in a clean hold.

The shocking news from downstream came to him in the canal-side pub. A Black Country boatman with a big voice was regaling the whole bar with news of the find. Ezra was intrigued. How had they found the body? He was not afraid.

He knew he was not caught. But he knew that the body could well now be connected with what had, until its discovery, been no more than a missing man in Birmingham.

He had always seen the landlord as the weak link in his scheme, but he had made sure that Benyon had no idea either how the murder had been done or, more importantly, where the body had been disposed of.

He had planned carefully and chosen the time and the spot with great precision. He travelled the route frequently and knew without doubt that the canal was both wide and deep before the Cowley Tunnel and bridge. He could not have been observed unless someone had been lying in wait to spy on him, and this was an absurd prospect. He knew, most importantly, that the canal had been thoroughly dredged at this spot, for only two months ago, he had had to wait half a day at the entrance to the tunnel while a backlog of southbound traffic passed him as he waited to go north.

While the garrulous man gave speculative details of the murder and drank at his listeners' expense, Ezra went over the details of the murder in his mind. He rehearsed in minute detail the dumping of the body on that morning three weeks ago.

They had left Nechells Wharf at dawn. The feckless youth, William, had sauntered up with the Shire from the near-by stables, and they had been hitched up and off down the black cinder paths through central Birmingham before five a.m.

At a steady two miles an hour they walked north out of Birmingham, hauling thirty tons of coal and a small dead man beneath the hold covers. Stopping only for tea and bacon and for the horse to feed, they left the Birmingham Main Line by mid-afternoon and joined the Shropshire Union at Autherley Junction, just north of Wolverhampton.

By dusk they had trudged up through Brewood and past

Stretton Aqueduct where it crosses the A5, through Wheaton Aston and up to the turnover bridge at Church Eaton. Here, they stopped. There was stabling and good mooring, and they were less than two miles from where Ezra planned to dispose of part of his cargo early the next morning. It was nearly nine o'clock when they had tied up the boat and bedded the horse down. They had travelled over twenty-five miles in their fifteen-hour day.

Ezra was well pleased with the distance that he had put between himself and his crime. But even as he lay in his bunk that night, the corpse of the man he had killed nestled in the hard coals just above his head.

The next day, at dawn, in an overcast early September, they were off again down the path. Within the hour they pulled in to the side and William led the horse away. There was no towpath through the tunnel and he would walk the horse over the hill and then return himself. The two men would then lie on their outriggers and quietly 'leg' the boat through the eighty-yard tunnel cut into the sandstone.

As soon as William was out of sight, Ezra hauled back the cover and exposed the corpse. With the body before him, he peered up and down the cut and across the fields on either side. Nothing was stirring. William was disappearing across to the other side of the bridge.

Ezra hauled the body out of the hold and bumped it down on to the deck. He stepped down on to the towpath and looked up and down again. It was not too late to re-conceal the body should anyone approach. Nothing. He pulled the corpse along the path, its progress halting and awkward. It caught on something just before the place where he was going to topple it into the water. It was a mooring spike. It caught and, as quickly, broke free.

He ran to the hold and collected the four bags of coal-weights in their little sacks and tied them roughly to Beech's neck and ankles. He looked up and down again; not a thing to be seen. Across the fields, only a magpie squawking. 'One for sorrow,' he said, as he put his boot against the bundle and rolled it in, the coals in their sacks bumping in after it.

CHAPTER 12

Detective-Inspector Hammond, who sometimes thought that he had seen it all before, hadn't quite seen it all. And, as he drove slowly back to Birmingham in his unmarked black Austin 9, he wished that he had not seen this body and, in particular, smelled it. Once the image—or in this case smell—entered the mind, he knew that there was no way of erasing it. Visions came to you in your sleep and woke you with sweating horror. The pictures presented themselves at the most uncomfortable times. Sitting little Emily on his lap on a Sunday afternoon after tea, he would recall a battered body, and the joy of his child would be tinged with fear and horror for her. Sometimes he would squeeze her to him too tightly and she would pull away embarrassed and wholly unaware of what her father was suddenly thinking. His wife had often woken in the night to find them smothered in their bed, his head bowed into her chest, his strong legs locked around her thighs, sweat pouring from him, the bed wet. She would try to ease his vice-like grip from her and dry his forehead as he came out of his nightmare with a start.

She never asked him what it was. She knew that it was some horror of his work and that he needed only to be held. The kindly, intelligent man would lie cradled in his wife's soft arms, his head rising and falling gently to the movement of her ample bosom.

The inquiry had begun at Beech's boarding-house. When he had not returned after three days, Mrs Pringle had walked into Hagley Road police station and, apologizing for her behaviour, said that she was worried about her missing lodger. It wasn't like him, she said, not to return. He was a man who always made arrangements, and he stuck to them. The desk sergeant took all the available details, but the landlady was unable to give him the name of a single friend or acquaintance, for he never brought anyone to his rooms. It wasn't that sort of establishment, she said. She knew, though, that it was at the Belle Vue Hotel, on Icknield Port Road, that he drank most frequently, he had never made any secret of that.

She leaned towards the sergeant and whispered that in her opinion she thought that he drank rather too much. But when he came in, even if it was late and he had had a lot to drink, he was always quiet and considerate; he always used the lavatory with care and she had never heard him stumble or fall. He paid his rent on the due day, not before, never after. He was a good lodger. Polite and courteous. He praised the food, which he always ate. In eighteen months she had never put a meal before him that he had not finished. She hoped that nothing had befallen him. She wouldn't wish to lose him.

The sergeant wondered if there was more to the missing lodger's relationship with his landlady than she was revealing. She was quite an attractive woman, and she hadn't mentioned a husband. It wouldn't be the first time that a landlady had done more for her lodger than make his bed and fry his breakfast. Perhaps he had simply gone off without telling her.

He would make inquiries, he promised her. He would make inquiries in the area and report back to her as soon as possible. She was grateful. She apologized for being foolish, if that proved to be the case, but it had got to the stage where she felt that she had to do something. The sergeant had heard it all before. He was delighted to help. It was what they were there for. She turned and he watched her walk away. Good legs. Perhaps the lodger had been enjoying the creature comforts of his landlady, he thought.

The sergeant began with a morning call at the Belle Vue. The landlord hadn't been open long when he came into the bar, but it was clear immediately that the policeman was conducting an entirely routine inquiry.

He said yes to a bottle of Brown Ale. Yes, Clifford knew Beech, he came in quite often. He didn't say that he was usually served by his wife. (He feared her response to any questions, and her appearance had gone from bad to worse in a matter of only three days.)

Clifford volunteered the information that he hadn't seen Beech for a few days. Was there anything wrong?

'Nothing wrong, I don't suppose,' said the policeman. 'He just hasn't been back to his lodgings for a day or two. Probably lady problems, you know.'

Clifford did know, but tried not to betray it. 'Travelling salesman, I think, wasn't he?' he said.

'Still is, I hope,' laughed the sergeant.

That was how easy it was, thought Clifford. One word. One careless word, a past tense instead of a present, and that could put a noose around your soft neck. When you told the truth it didn't matter how often you told the story, because it was true. You couldn't slip and stumble and give yourself away. If you were lying, though, they kept on at you, over and over, until you made one little error, and then they prised and teased and winkled away until the little crack was a gap, a gap that they could get a wedge into, and then they pushed and forced and levered you open until you were all spilled out. Just from that one little slip.

'Is your wife in this morning?' asked the sergeant.

'She is, but she's not been well for a day or two, I'm afraid, Sergeant. She's resting upstairs.'

'Nothing serious, I hope, sir,' said the policeman, as he poured the rest of his beer into the tilted glass.

'She seems . . . she seems to have 'flu or something like it. She feels very tired, and no appetite.'

'Has she had the doctor in?' asked the sergeant, apparently with more interest in the glass of dark brown beer held out to the light in front of him than in the landlord's wife in bed upstairs.

'She says she won't. You know what these women can be like. Are you married . . . ?'

'I know exactly what they're like. Twenty-two years this July. That's how much I know about them, at least one of them, and that's enough for me.' He tipped the beer back and wiped his lips with the back of his hand. The two men walked towards the door.

'This Beech fellow, any particular friends? Drinking companions, anyone like that who might have an idea of his whereabouts?' asked the sergeant as they stood at the door.

'He was friendly with quite a few of the men in the smokeroom,' said Clifford. 'Seemed to be quite popular in there.'

'And what did you make of him, sir?' asked the policeman as he pulled on his helmet.

It was an afterthought, and asked in such a relaxed way that Clifford was almost lured into replying honestly: he was a bastard, a show-off, an arrogant Yorkshire bastard who cuckolded me and caused me untold misery. He gathered himself. 'He was all right. He liked a drink and a chat, a singsong at the piano. In this trade you have to get on with everybody. You can't pick and choose who walks through the door. They're all customers.'

'Very true, sir. Very true and very sensible. Well, thank you for the beer and I'll be on my way. If anything turns up, I'll let you know or send one of the boys round. If he calls in here and doesn't appear to know he's even a missing person, mention it to him and ask him to call in at the station, would you? Stranger things have happened. Memory loss. Amnesia I think it's called. Covers a multitude of excuses! Never worked for me when I've tried it with my missus, I can tell you.' He grinned and strolled off down the road.

CHAPTER 13

The discovery of a body, as opposed to an inquiry about a missing person, brought the police back to Mrs Pringle's boarding-house in Gillott Road. They now wanted to know exactly what the nature of the relationship between the landlady and her lodger had been. The Inspector was not over-delicate in seeking to satisfy himself absolutely that there had been no impropriety between the couple. Had there been so, there was always the possibility of a third party, of jealousy, of disagreement of one sort or another, and this could lead anywhere, as the Inspector's service in the force had shown him time and time again.

But he didn't feel that there had been anything between these two. Beech was, by all accounts, a gregarious man; she was an attractive woman in her early forties. She had lost her husband in France at the very close of the Great War. She had been twenty-eight at the time. She had never married again, cherishing the memory of her late husband, lamenting the family that she was never destined to have, and not, apparently, showing anything but a purely professional interest in her paying guests.

Even had the Inspector's sensitive nose picked up a faint scent of wrongdoing, the rest of the crime made no sense. The man's body weighted down in a canal thirty miles away? No, it didn't make sense. Amateur, impulse murders were hastily performed and bungled in every imaginable way. They left trails of clues a yard wide that a child could follow. And anyway, there was always a sign, a bit of gossip, someone who drew back the curtain when they perhaps shouldn't have done, and who saw something that they could always be persuaded to tell a policeman. It was the rule of the playground, not the law of the jungle. It was often pure unalloyed spite that led someone to tell on some-one else, nothing to do with altruism or moral upstand-ingness.

The Inspector then drove to Beech's employer in central Birmingham. Jessop's Surgical Supplies had been visited before, but it was the Inspector's first call on the proprietor.

The premises were unprepossessing: up three grey floors in an ill-lit warren of offices and storerooms in dingy Marti-neau Street. The story was unexceptionable, too. Beech had been so successful in Yorkshire that he had been promoted to the Midlands. He was a very good salesman and there were big markets to be exploited between here and Oxford in the south and up to Crewe in the north. He was ex-ploiting those markets. He had had three salary increases in the eighteen months that he had been down here and his commission was the highest of the entire sales force.

He would be sorely missed, said a sallow and undemon-strative Mr Jessop, 'Sorely missed.'

'And did he have any enemies?' the Inspector wanted to know.

'Is it possible to be in business and not make enemies?' answered the manufacturer laconically.

'Of course. But real enemies. Anyone who would wish to harm him? Really harm him?' said the Inspector with emphasis, remembering the body on the towpath.

'There must have been people that he had offended in getting our ranges into shops and stores, but people don't normally kill for that kind of thing, do they? At least not in surgical supplies, as far as I am aware.'

Something that the Inspector had not been able to put his finger on, but that he had been faintly aware of since he came into the little office on the third floor, became clear to him in that one sarcastic aside: Jessop was, of course, homosexual. His demeanour and bearing were stating it so clearly that the Inspector was concerned that he hadn't picked it up as soon as he had met the man ten minutes ago.

The Inspector conjectured that there would have been no love lost between these two: the outgoing Yorkshireman and the slightly effeminate manufacturer of surgical goods and appliances. But the questioning led nowhere. Jessop knew nothing. He had lost his best salesman, but was apparently unmoved by his violent death.

After twenty minutes, with the Inspector perched on a cardboard box of surgical corsets, and the manufacturer using his toes to swivel slightly in a grey metal chair before him, the Inspector called it a day. Jessop remained seated as he watched the policeman go.

As the days became weeks, Mary's mother virtually disappeared from family and business life. When Mary passed her on the landing, she hardly spoke. She had a shawl wrapped about her nightdress and looked down at the child as if unsure of who she was. Mary was astonished. She knew that something was dreadfully wrong and had, with a combination of duty and inquisitiveness, asked her father what it was. He had fumbled and stumbled an answer which amounted to a kindly, 'I can't tell you.' As all that Mary had ever looked for, and ever failed to get from her mother, was precisely this quality of kindness, she inquired no longer.

She was still immensely curious about the profound changes that had taken place but, seeing that her own situation had improved immeasurably, she was herself not unhappy. Since her mother's withdrawal, she had been allowed to play with a schoolfriend who lived down the road, had even stayed there for tea one Saturday afternoon and walked back pretending that she was a little girl who went and had tea with friends every week of the year.

Last Saturday morning, she had made her father a cup of coffee with milk and carried it to him with great concentration as he stood behind the big bar that she could barely see over. She spent more time out of her bedroom and in the now largely unoccupied family kitchen and parlour. She imagined all sorts of things. She pretended that she was the lady of the house, and that she told Annie what to buy for supper and where to clean today and what to cook. In fact, Annie had walked into the kitchen quietly one morning and heard Mary acting out her fantasy. She had given her a very severe look which made the girl leave the room and avoid the older woman for the rest of the morning.

Sitting at her bedroom window one evening, as the light faded and the noise from the bar and the smoke-room rose and the boots chafed across the yard to the Gents in the corner, she remembered that she hadn't seen her friend Mr Beech for what seemed like ages. She still had the sixpence piece that he had thrown to her. She was a thrifty girl and was saving for a farm set that was in the toy shop in Edward Street. She looked at it every day on her way home from school. It was four and elevenpence. The owner had accepted her shilling deposit, and now she was saving for the remaining three and elevenpence. Mr Beech's sixpence was in her money-box with all of her other pennies. Her thoughts catapulted from her mother to her father to Beech to the farm set and the toy-shop owner's grumpy wife and how in *Mary's* world no one would be allowed to sell lovely blue-and-yellow boxes of brightly coloured toys, buses and cars and vans, dolls and soldiers and trains, balls and kites and marbles, unless they were *really* nice to all the children all the time, and not just when their mothers and fathers were in the shop with them.

She heard her mother padding down the dark landing to the bathroom, but she let her thoughts drift and imagined

herself back in the toy-shop window snuggled down to the
kennel that housed the farm dog. She rearranged the lovely
dun fencing and its swinging five-bar gate, worked the
man's arm that grasped his thin piece of wire that was a
shepherd's crook, the other arm cradling a lamb slung over
his shoulder, and in her mind she lay down at the little
mirror that formed the green-edged duck pond and brought
the cattle nearer to the edge to drink and saw the ducks
glide away as, from behind the green elm trees in a cluster
at the corner, rode the gentleman on his chestnut mare, the
man who could one day be squire and one day a farmer,
and one day . . . She climbed into bed, gently and carefully,
and didn't kneel to say her prayers but held the memory of
her toy dream and let it lie about her as she slipped quietly
into sleep.

CHAPTER 14

After the previous afternoon's visit to Jessop's Surgical Supplies, with its acrid smell of dry boxes, padding and lint, belts and trusses, elastic and pills, it was a relief for the Inspector to drive out to Five Ways on Saturday morning with the window of his car wound down.

He drove past the deserted cricket ground at Edgbaston, deliberately making a little detour to do so. He had seen very little cricket this summer: on the rare occasions that he had been free to watch for a few hours, the rain had fallen or the light faded before he could take his seat. But as he drove around the high, red-brick walls he recalled clearly the glorious day that he had spent there with two friends in the summer of 1929 when England had played South Africa. Curiously, although the cricket had been marvellous, it was not the game that the Inspector remembered, but the smell of that day. The whole experience lay in his memory as the smell of the heavy cream canvas of the beer tent, the pint of Mitchell's and Butler's dark frothy mild in his hand, the sun warming through the big tent and mixing with the heady fumes of trodden grass, warm beer, and an English summer.

The Inspector sat outside the Belle Vue in his black Austin. He had parked around the corner from the hotel (a grand name for a rather ordinary pub, he thought) so that he could sit in the late September sun for a few minutes longer.

He didn't want to go in and talk to the landlord and his wife yet. He pushed back into the brown-leather seat and felt the sun on his face. The draycart pulled in through the big, backyard gates. He lit a Capstan Full Strength and watched as the draymen began dexterously to spin the barrels off their cart and on to the big coconut mats with a dull thump.

A few minutes later the landlord appeared at the back door, his sleeves rolled up and his collar open at the stud. He was a fair-haired man in his early thirties, but he had a slight stoop, the sort of round shoulders belonging to a much older man. He spoke a word or two to the draymen and went into the shadows again.

The Inspector was becoming uncomfortably hot. There was no breeze and the sun was already high in the blue sky over Birmingham. Perhaps a drink would be nice. He'd never been into a pub on an inquiry without being offered a drink by the landlord, even if, three months and a detailed investigation later, he had had the man sent away for five years for fraud or arson or theft.

He walked round to the front of the hotel. The doors were open and there were two people in the bar, both reading racing papers. One looked up and immediately returned to his form guide. The other did not stir.

The Inspector introduced himself with a question at the bar: 'Clifford Benyon?'

The man was taken aback. 'Yes. Can I help you?'

'I'm Detective-Inspector Hammond of Birmingham City Police. It's about a missing person.' He flipped open his notebook. He knew the name but he had learned to use these little pauses to see how the person being questioned filled them. 'A Mr . . . Thomas Beech.'

'I spoke to a sergeant about it. He was here about two weeks ago asking me if I knew him. I told him all I know. Have you found him, then?'

'Well, in a sense we have,' said the Inspector, leaving the pause as long as he reasonably might. 'What I mean to say is, if we had found him and everything was all right, well,

frankly, I wouldn't be here. I'm sure you can see that, sir.'
He waited. He wanted a response.

'Well, yes, I suppose so. So what do you mean? You have
found him, but there's something wrong?'

'Yes, there is.' The Inspector had been questioning for so
long now that he couldn't always tell when he was making
genuine inquiries and when he was honing his technique,
playing games to improve his methods. He had absolutely
no suspicions about Clifford, but he was questioning him
as though he had. The Inspector's wife, Bethan, had actually had to reprimand him for doing it to her on occasions
recently: 'Where is the weeding fork?' Pause. 'Are you absolutely certain that you didn't have it after I put it back in
the shed?' Pause.

'John, can you hear yourself?' she had said. 'I haven't
committed any crime with the weeding fork. It has simply
gone astray. Things do. Perhaps Emily took it out into the
garden to play with.'

'Of course, dear, I'm sorry. Bringing my work home with
me again.' He had patted her backside and thanked heaven
for her Welsh common sense and genuine good nature.

Clifford was looking at him blankly. 'Well, Inspector?
What is "wrong" with him?'

'I'm afraid he's dead, sir.' The emptiness of this statement was accentuated by the Inspector's flat Birmingham
accent.

Clifford looked directly at the Inspector and then turned
towards the line of spirits bottles behind him. The Inspector
could see his face in the mirror with its frosted scrollwork
extolling the virtues of India Pale Ale. Clifford poured himself a whisky, turned to the soda bottle on the counter, and
controlled a splash into the glass.

'What can I get you, Inspector?'

'Thank you, sir. I'll have a glass of beer, if I may.'

Clifford poured him a glass of bitter, held it up to the

light, the first drawing that day, acknowledged it fit and handed it to the policeman.

'I just don't know what to say,' said Clifford. 'Why would anyone want to do anything to him?'

'I beg your pardon, sir?'

'Beech. Why would anyone want to do anything to him? Something like this.'

'Like what, sir?'

'Well, whatever's happened to him.'

'But I didn't say that anything had happened to him, Mr Benyon.' There was a hint of severity in the use of the name. A word of caution forbidding familiarity.

'You said that he was dead. I'm assuming that something tragic has befallen him. He was a young man. Am I wrong?'

'I'm afraid that you're only too right, sir. He has been found murdered.'

Clifford was relieved to serve a customer while the Inspector stood alone and sipped his beer.

The Inspector thought that he rather liked Clifford. He ran a nice quiet pub, even if its calling itself a hotel smacked of a little pretentiousness. There was a nice atmosphere in the quiet bar that autumn Saturday morning. The drinkers came in quietly and politely. A beer and the racing page here, a chat between chums standing at the bar there. A man on his way home from a late-night shift dropping in for something to see him off when he tried to sleep during the warm day.

The Inspector was an ideal copper. He imagined a story and hung one on every person that crossed his path. The lives that he gave people were usually infinitely more interesting than those that they actually lived. He knew as well, from hard experience, that what people chose to show of themselves was a very small part of the whole, was certainly a very small part of anything which could be called 'the truth'.

At eleven o'clock a sweet girl of seven or eight pushed open the door from the upstairs apartments and very carefully walked through with a cup of milky coffee and a digestive biscuit on a little wooden tray. All her concentration was on the task in hand, and it wasn't until the door rocked to behind her that she looked up at her father and saw his unusual companion. 'Here's your coffee, Daddy. Can I go out and play now, please?'

'Say good morning to the Inspector, Mary. Inspector, this is my daughter, Mary.'

'Hello, Mary. How are you today?' said the Inspector.

The little girl looked up at the smartly dressed man, but said nothing in reply.

'Would you like some coffee, Inspector?' asked Clifford. The Inspector drained his glass and held it a little way from him. Clifford knew all the different ways in which customers suggested that it was time for another drink. 'Perhaps you'd prefer another glass, Inspector? It's going to be a warm day, I think.'

'Thank you, Mr Benyon, that'd be very acceptable.' There was the name again, but this time it signalled the cessation of further sparring.

Mary was waiting for an answer, though her father had forgotten that there had been a question.

'You'd better go and play now, Mary. I have to speak to the Inspector. Be good now, off you go.'

'Nice little girl,' said the policeman as she shut the door. 'I have one the same age, perhaps a little older. My Emily's just gone nine. But let's get back to Beech, if we may, sir. Tell me, did he have any particular friends in the pu . . . hotel?'

'He seemed to get on with everyone, very popular man as far as I could tell,' replied the landlord.

'What do you mean: "As far as you could tell"—didn't you like him?'

'Yes, I liked him all right, but I didn't serve him that often, he tended to drink in the smoke-room.'

'Oh yes, I suppose he would have done. And who served him in there?'

Was Clifford wrong or had that little trap been set and sprung by the policeman? Had the Inspector made the words come out of his mouth? He had to lie or say the word. The seconds were passing. 'My wife. She serves in the smoke-room usually.'

The Inspector craned his neck in a theatrical fashion towards the empty smoke-room.

'Is she not working at the moment, sir?'

'She's not been well for a few days. I've taken on someone else, hired a barman temporarily.'

The Inspector looked at his notepad.

'Of course, it's here. You told the sergeant your wife wasn't well. But it's longer than you think, sir. It's nearly three weeks. Yes, the date's here. He spoke to you on the Friday, three days after Mr Beech had disappeared, and your wife had been unwell for a day or two then. She's been poorly nearly three weeks, sir.'

'Do you policemen write down everything? I only mentioned in passing that my wife wasn't well and it's all there in black and white, in police records.'

'Just details, sir. At the beginning of any inquiry, you have no idea what may prove to be significant by the end.'

There was a long pause.

'What seems to be the trouble with your wife, sir?'

'It's difficult to say, Inspector. One of those ladies' things I think, rather personal.'

'Of course, Mr Benyon. I'm sorry. I shouldn't have asked. Better left with the experts, eh?'

'Yes, I think so,' said the landlord.

There was another pause.

'When did the doctor see her, sir? It says here that she

had decided not to see him when my sergeant spoke to you?'
Clifford had been cornered. This was the way in which
they trapped you. Innocent interest and concern, easy talk,
familiar and friendly even, and then you were caught.

'She hasn't seen the doctor. She won't see him. She's not
well, but she won't see the doctor, you know what women
are like, they won't be told.'

'And are you managing, sir? Are you coping? With your
daughter, and the pub? There must be staff to see to and a
lot to organize in a pub, or a hotel, rather?'

'I am managing. I have a . . . we have a lady, Anna, who
helps upstairs, and Mary is very good, and I've got a decent
enough chappie in the bar to help me. But what has all this
got to do with Beech? My affairs aren't really helping that
matter.'

Your 'affairs', thought the Inspector. Are you, Mr
Benyon, he wondered, having an affair? Who is the woman
Anna that 'helps upstairs'? Is that why your wife is in bed
and not wishing to see a doctor or anyone else? Are you
keeping people from her so that she cannot shame you?

'You're right, of course,' said the Inspector briskly. 'Poor
Mr Beech is the man that we should all be thinking about
at present. But I do hope that your wife feels a little better
soon. It would be helpful if I could have a chat with her.
She used to serve in the smoke-room. Beech drank there.
She may have seen something, noticed something. Women
are so much better at these things than we are, don't you
agree, sir?'

It was not really a question and Clifford didn't bother to
answer. Personally, he had always thought that his own
powers of observation were infinitely better than Gertie's
and, for that matter, those of just about every other woman
that he had ever known. However, this was no time for
discussion of that sort. And he was keen for the Inspector
to leave as soon as possible. He had been unnerved by him

twice in their half-hour together. Another five minutes and he felt that he might confess the whole thing to him.

'As soon as she's well enough. I'll make sure that you know straight away, Inspector.'

'Meanwhile, if you don't mind, Mr Benyon, I'll have someone come down and chat to the regulars, see if anyone noticed anything unusual, any strange faces about the place, that kind of thing. We'll be discreet, but these things have to be done. They'll be reading about it in the paper pretty soon anyway. We've kept it out so far—didn't want everyone establishing their alibis, you know.' He laughed. 'Right, sir, I'd better be off, plenty to do, not enough time to do it in. Give my regards to your wife, and I hope that we won't have to trouble you too much in the future.'

'Inspector . . .'

'Yes, sir?'

'You haven't said . . . you haven't told me . . .'

'Told you how he died, Mr Benyon . . .'

There was the name again, but this time its use could have meant anything at all: unfriendly? accusatory? neutral?

'Oh, usual sort of thing. Head bashed in. Nothing extraordinary. Body was in a strange spot, though. In a cut. Tied up and thrown in a cut. We were lucky to find it. Whoever did this came close to getting away with it. No body. No murder. But we'll get him now. Always do once we've got the body. No wallet. Suggestion of robbery. All his cash gone. But it wasn't for the loot. They left his watch and ring, both worth quite a bit. Worried about identification, you see. An ordinary thief wouldn't be. Not enough at stake. What they *should've* done is taken the jewellery but got rid of it straight away, chucked it in a river or something. That would have thrown us for a bit.'

He paused and looked down thoughtfully into his glass. 'But of course, they didn't expect us to find the body, did they? And there's the rub. They just don't think these things through. They make one mistake, more if we're lucky, one's enough though, and we're on to them.' He banged his pint pot on to the counter at the last word and Clifford started.

'Body in the water for a couple of weeks, not a sight you'd wish to see, I can assure you, sir. Wish I hadn't seen it myself, to be honest. Well, good morning. I'll be seeing you again, no doubt.'

He turned as he got to the open doors and stood with his back to the full sunlight. 'Lovely pint of bitter, that, I look forward to seeing you in altogether happier circumstances. Good day to you, Mr Benyon.'

CHAPTER 15

Ezra sat at the stern of *Crow* with the great rudder crooked under his arm. The boat maintained a steady course down the cut as the angle at which he held it countered exactly that of the horse's tendency to pull the boat not only along, but actually into the towpath.

He had a great deal on his mind as he sat there watching scrawny William's thin frame jolt along with none of the rhythm of the seventeen-hand Shire at his side. The great piebald animal planted its giant hooves with the steady progress of one entirely superior to the ignominy of its task.

Ezra had gone over the murder and the dumping of the body endlessly, but in two days' time they would be repassing the spot and perhaps there would be a clue to its discovery there. Would there still be a police presence, he wondered. How long after a crime was the scene of the deed returned to the common lot?

He had become fanatical about *Crow*. The interior he had scoured, first with his eyes, over and over again, methodically squaring it out in his mind and covering a section at a time. And then, when this was done and there was nothing to be seen anyway, he went over it with his pail and cloth and stiff-bristled brush. Every time that William was at the stables, or sent for bread, or was walking the horse over a bridge or tunnel before they legged the boat through, Ezra would be at the cabin walls and floor again. There was no clue left there. He didn't stop his ritualistic and obsessive cleaning of the place, but he knew that nothing here could lead anyone to him.

What he knew he had to do, though, was to return, as normal, to the Belle Vue. Although afraid of this unknown, he knew that he had to deal with whatever trap might be laid.

But could Benyon cope? Had he already collapsed and blurted out the conspiracy under the first little pressure that had probably been brought to bear on him?

If the salesman had been traced to Birmingham, and from his lodgings there to the pub that he drank at, how long before they would find out about his relationship with the landlord's wife? Soon; of that Ezra felt sure.

They would find that Benyon had a motive. But they would also see, if they had any sense, that he clearly lacked the wherewithal to kill.

The next question was crucial: was there any connection between himself and Beech? There was not. Had anyone ever seen them together? They had not.

They might connect him with the canals. They might well know that he and the murdered man drank at the same pub. But that was all they could know.

They certainly couldn't pin murder on him.

The money, the two hundred and fifty pounds from Benyon, was hidden where no one would ever find it. He would have to beware of how, and if, he accepted the other half of the money, in case the publican had cracked and this was the method that they were going to use to try and trap him. But he would be able to tell if he had cracked as soon as he walked into the pub, of this he felt sure.

This visit to the pub he had to make, and he had to do it well. While they might not be able to prove his guilt, it was even better if they thought him innocent.

CHAPTER 16

Gertie sat at the dressing-table in what had become her room alone, and toyed with her make-up things. She had not been told yet of the discovery of Beech's body. But she knew that something dreadful had befallen him. He was not the sort of man to disappear. She reluctantly acknowledged that he thought too much of himself to allow any sort of anonymity to overtake him. She knew it was a less than kindly thought, but it was true.

And Clifford had changed, of course. He appeared to be functioning within himself, communicating nothing of his feelings. He must be involved with Thomas's disappearance, the coincidence was too much. They were playing a waiting game; he was waiting for her to accuse him of complicity in the disappearance of her lover. She was not going to give him the satisfaction. She would withdraw. From him, from family life and from her work downstairs in the hotel.

What had he done, though? She puzzled and thought and slept with the question in her mind and woke with it there but mixed anew with the skein of her dreams. Clifford must have frightened him in some way. Perhaps he had paid some brute to frighten away her lover. Or had he paid him some enormous sum to go away to another part of the country, or the world? Would Thomas have accepted? Could Clifford have done it? And where would he get the kind of money that could 'buy' a man like Tom? He earned more than Clifford ever would. He had 'investments', he had a new car, several nice suits, lots of shoes. Clifford had none of these things. He dithered endlessly about them buying a car. Their few savings were in the bank in Temple

Row, exactly as they had always been. Clifford lacked the imagination to engineer the disappearance of her man. So what had happened?

She fingered the glass face-powder jar in front of her and lifted the lid, patted the puff up and down in the pink powder and watched the little clouds of dust as they rose and fell. In the half-light of the afternoon, the curtains of the bedroom drawn against the sun, she looked at herself in the mirrors. The wing mirrors gave a comprehensive picture of her face, right round to the side of her neck. She was a miserable sight: her eyes deep-set, her cheekbones prominent; her hair hadn't been washed for more days than she cared to remember; she hadn't bathed. Her pink bedroom shawl accentuated the picture of her decrepitude; she looked ten years older than her thirty-three years.

She took the powder-puff and flapped it at the central mirror, patting away the image of her face, ring after ring of powder smudging away the reflection of herself. When the mirror was covered she looked to one side and then the other and saw herself still there, the same pathetic sight. She cradled her head in her folded arms and lay down among the debris of her dressing-table, the fat tears rolling down her cheeks.

That evening the Inspector returned. He had said that someone would call, but now he was here himself, with his big sergeant, and both of them sitting in the Inspector's car in plain clothes. As Clifford opened the doors of the pub at six o'clock, the Inspector's ingenuous smile met him. He returned a hollow greeting.

No sooner had the first customers walked through the door than the Inspector and the sergeant followed them. The sergeant came and ordered them both pints of bitter, Clifford waved away the ten-shilling note, 'Please, on the house.' But it was a mirthless gift.

As the customers took their seats, one or other of the policemen went and sat near them, introduced himself discreetly and started to chat in that easy, disarming style that Clifford had already witnessed. The Inspector worked in the smoke-room, as befitted his higher status, the sergeant in the bar. Sometimes they would talk to one customer, sometimes to a group of two or three friends together. The regulars seemed to be enjoying the experience, there was laughter and the rounds of drinks included one for the policemen. Then, amid the jollity, there was a pause, a silence from the group, and grave and serious expressions replaced those of moments ago.

The Inspector had hit them for six. Beech was dead, been found murdered a few days ago. The man that they had been ready to chat about was dead. Just as Clifford had found himself drawn in, so too had these men. They had been lured into being candid about the missing man.

The Inspector knew exactly what he was doing. Having committed themselves in this way, they would now need to retreat and recant, clear themselves of any suggestion of involvement, no matter how remote, with the death of a man whom none of them really liked. The Inspector knew that there was probably not a man among them who could be involved, but it might throw up a shred of information that he could use. At the very least it might help to fill in some of the background on the murdered man.

They had spoken lightly, but they had spoken a little ill, of the dead. They had said nothing dreadful, but they had made playful suggestions of his being a bit of a ladies' man, of his having plenty of money and standing far too many rounds. That he always talked Yorkshire cricket and had some new dirty jokes, was good at the piano, had shown them some fruity postcards, was one of the boys and, most surprising of all, that to a man they didn't really like him.

'You're right about that,' chimed in the Inspector. 'Someone didn't like him at all.'

But no one in the little group was willing, especially with Clifford standing a few yards away from them, to intimate what some of them suspected was the true nature of the relationship between Gertrude and the murdered man.

The fact that Clifford's involvement in a murder was beyond the comprehension of any of them also ensured their present silence.

Jack Ollier went to the bar for the next round. All the men asked for whisky. Beer in deep pint glasses no longer seemed appropriate to the situation. The landlord said to Jack, 'He's told you then, has he?'

'You already knew, Clifford?' said the insurance man in reply.

'I knew when he told me this afternoon, but he told me not to say anything. It's the way they do the inquiries, apparently.'

'Strikes me as plain bloody crafty,' said the aggrieved Ollier.

He wanted to ask if Clifford's wife had heard the news and, if so, how she had taken it. But it was too direct. Jack could not ask the other man such a question. He took the whiskies on the small tray and returned to the serious group in the corner.

The Inspector had counselled them to discretion until he had had the opportunity to speak to everyone in the smoke-room that evening. He couldn't expect people to hold the information once they got out, and therefore he had only one evening among the regulars. It wasn't beyond the pale of reason that word could have already made its way from the canal to these parts by one route or another, but, given that few people outside the police force knew the identity of the body, it was unlikely.

Next door, in the bar, the sergeant was also making some

progress. Here, little whisky was drunk and, even after he revealed that the missing man was now a murdered man, the atmosphere could not have been described as grave, but rather as excited.

The men wanted the details. Most of them knew of Beech, had stood next to him in the dark urinal, heard his big laughter through the mahogany and glass screen. They'd heard the piano often enough, and knew him to be the player. But they knew little more of him. None of them knew that he had been involved with the landlord's wife.

Did the locals know of anyone with a grudge against Beech? Had he been seen with anyone unusual? Had there been any strangers in the bar recently?

In the charged and heady atmosphere, the regulars speculated about the only drinkers who were not well known to them.

One or two strangers were identified, but there was no real consensus. Certainly, in a pub not two miles from the centre of Birmingham, there had been strangers who had called for an evening, sometimes only for a pint or two, and had then never been seen again.

But one or other of the regulars knew most of the occasional callers. When Talbot was recalled and described, several of the men knew of him.

'Sits there,' gestured one to the table by the far window.

'Never heard him say a word,' said another.

'Got a bit of a limp—gammy leg,' said Arthur.

'How often does he come by?' eased the sergeant, smelling a faint scent in an otherwise barren field.

Shrugs of the shoulders. But as they looked from one to another, two or three weeks was suggested.

'What does he do?' asked the sergeant, concealing his interest in an expressionless voice.

'No idea,' replied first one, then another.

'Has he been in lately?' asked the policeman.

'I haven't seen him for a bit,' said Walter Simmonds, the butcher.

Accounts differed, but no one thought that the man had been in for a few weeks.

'Did anyone ever see this fellow talking to Beech?'

No one had. The scent was wafting away.

When the sergeant and the Inspector compared notes in the smoke-filled car outside the pub after closing time that evening, they agreed that while this occasional visitor was not a very promising line of inquiry, he was virtually their only one. Perhaps he was a traveller of some sort if he only came by every few weeks. It was too much to hope that he was what they both desperately wanted: someone with a connection with canals.

Perhaps the drink helped, but as they sat in the car, a bit tipsy from the beers and whiskies, and rather tired from the long day, they both felt just a slight sense of anticipation in tracking down this rather mysterious figure who might just be able to throw a little light on the inquiry.

Would he return to the pub? If he didn't return, it made his activities even more suspect. They would then have to find him, arrest him and break him down under questioning. Easier said than done, but if he was a bargeman, if he had habits, he probably had to keep to them: work schedules, accommodation, contracts, deliveries, anything, and they would find him. But if the canal connection was a wild hope, then the man could be anywhere.

If he did return, they would interrogate him. If he was sensible *and* guilty, he would return knowing that there would be an onslaught awaiting him. But he would be prepared for it. If—if, that was—he knew that the body had been found.

Their minds were racing like excited schoolboys. The man was probably an innocent traveller with a comprehen-

sive alibi for the period in question. He was probably a
respected family man whose wife would vouch for his
whereabouts every evening of the weeks around the time of
the murder.

But if so, why was he in this so-called hotel every few
weeks? Did she know about that? Was he visiting a lady
somewhere? They raced on through the possibilities.

The Inspector lit a Capstan from the stub of the one that
was still glowing between his fingers. The sergeant waited,
but the brown packet was not proffered. He took a Wood-
bine from his packet of ten and lit it, the smoke pouring
out of the window where he had opened it a few inches.

Clifford had rushed upstairs as soon as they had left. He
was standing in the darkness behind the closed curtains of
the upper front room, watching the smoke funnel away.

Gertie had cried herself to sleep on her dressing-table
top. She woke aching and red-faced. The face powder had
smeared and congealed about her. She climbed into her
unmade bed and curled up foetally. The whole pub downstairs now knew that her lover was dead. She knew it too,
but no one had told her.

CHAPTER 17

As *Crow* approached the place where the body had been dumped, Talbot became quietly excited. Pulling round the long gentle curve, he saw the tunnel ahead. It cut through a bed of sandstone rock a hundred yards wide and, on the other side, not three weeks ago, he had rolled into the still, dark waters the man whom he had bludgeoned to death two nights earlier.

As they drew up to the north entrance to the tunnel the two men went through their familiar silent routine. William called the horse to a halt, and the boat's momentum drew it up and into the side of the cut where it would moor. The younger man unhitched the towing-line at the harness and started off on his walk over the hill. William's hand clasped the rein and he walked along at the horse's side, deftly avoiding the huge beast's hooves.

The Shire seemed unaware of its freedom from its great burden and kept the same measured pace as it climbed away from the canal up the steep path. The boatman poured water into the kettle from one of the two cans that rode on the top of the craft and brewed tea. He sat astern in his usual position, arm crooked at the rudder, his grey spiky hair and weather-beaten face making him a formidable sight.

When William returned from walking the horse over the tunnel, the older man had a keen desire to ask him what he had seen on the other side. Was there still a police presence? Was there any evidence of the crime that had been discovered there? But William said nothing and Ezra resisted the strong temptation to ask him. He stepped on board, poured tea for himself from the battered pot and swilled it down. It was nearly cold.

The two men placed their lying planks in position and then William hauled the craft slowly up to the mouth of the tunnel. Passage through its length was supposed to be controlled on a time system, as in all tunnels: journeys from the northern end could only be begun on the half-hour, and from the southern entrance on the hour, and in this way disputes were supposed to be avoided. They were frequent. Many boat-owners did not possess a watch; some could not tell the time. Many claimed to have started their passage through the tunnels at the stated times when they clearly had not done so.

In a recent incident, the story of which had travelled the canals of the Midlands within a week, two boats had met in the middle of the dark, half-mile-long Gosty Hill Tunnel on the Dudley canal. After some initial skirmishing, in which a little sacrificial blood was spilt on the prow of both boats, the two crews, a total of three men, a woman, two children and two dogs, sat tight and prepared for a long siege. The owner of the Number One, travelling across from Nuneaton, had no rear-guard support, whereas the Company boat, travelling south from Wolverhampton, had supplies sent up the tunnel by a little butty boat. After a token resistance of another hour, and much verbal abuse, the privately owned boat was legged back the quarter-mile that it had come, and allowed the Company craft to pass with no very good grace. The dogs snarled and the crews swore vehemently as the craft passed one another at the tunnel's mouth, their eyes blinking as, after their long stay in the gloomy dark, they found themselves out in the daylight once more.

In the short tunnel, Ezra could see that no other craft was under way. The two men lay flat on their boards, their heads propped slightly on the centre rails, a piece of sacking protecting their necks from the roughest edges of the wood.

Rhythmically, steadily, silently they trod along the soft

sandstone walls, the dank smell growing as they advanced towards the centre. The men worked in a silent harmony that belied the paucity of friendship in their relationship.

As the stealthy craft made its quiet way through the dark hole, the only sounds were those of a rat swimming through the water or running up the brickwork out of the way of the craft, and the amplified drips of water that had seeped through the rock and now fell from the roof and plopped into the slowly swirling canal.

No matter how often these journeys were undertaken, and on some stretches they had to encounter two or three tunnels a day, it was always a relief to emerge unscathed at the other end. There were accidents: there had been roof falls and there was the occasional drowning—someone banging his head and falling in or being dragged along and smashed between boat and wall or bottom. Ezra himself constantly carried his own iron reminder of his childhood trauma, but, for the most part, it was simply a primæval fear of the dark: the coffin-like sense of isolation and darkness, the gradual shutting out of the light, like a lid slowly closing on you in this elongated place. Everyone was glad to emerge at the other end. The boat dogs often howled in the middle of the tunnel and, re-entering the light, ran up and down the length of the boat, demented.

Had it been a dream? There was nothing to see. No sign of crime. Had Ezra imagined it? Had that fool in the pub outside Tarporley told of another murder? It was beyond belief. He had named the spot. Ezra couldn't have imagined that. And yet here they were. On the very bank opposite them there must have been police and all the tools that they used: sheets and boxes and bits of scientific things to try and understand the crimes and the evidence; but now, nothing. Was it imagination, or were those brambles perhaps a little pushed down where a body might have lain, or some-one sat? He knew it was the exact place. He looked across at the old iron spike, dangerous at night, he thought, you could fall on it. Most posts these days were thick timber, more easily seen, less sharp for man and horse to gash themselves on.

William untied the placid, munching horse and the line was re-attached to the prow. As they drew away, Ezra looked back at the spot, at the tunnel and the bridge that ran over the end of it. He saw nothing. He fetched up a big piece of phlegm and gobbed it into the ripples that formed in their wake.

It was dusk when they tied up at the wharf at Nechells in Birmingham the following day. It was the very end of September and the nights were drawing in. But even at this hour barges were unloading and shifting cargoes beneath the gas lamps' flickering glow.

William dealt with the horse while Ezra checked the hold-covers. The load of cotton that they were carrying would be easily damaged by rain. Tomorrow they would unload, it was too late to begin now.

When William returned in half an hour he gathered his one or two possessions and stood there aimlessly, waiting to be paid.

Ezra felt contrary. 'What is it?' he said, coiling rope and not looking up. The other man was silent, but shifted in his boots. 'Are you off, then?' said Ezra. He was being cruel. The other man made to speak, but only a low sound emerged. 'You want your money, eh?' said Ezra. 'What you going to spend it on tonight, then? Going off with one of those whores again?'

He was enjoying himself with the near mute. But already he'd gone too far. William made to leave. Would he go without his money, Ezra wondered. He looked up. William was looking at him with ill-concealed hatred. Ezra had rarely seen this before. 'Wait, I've got your lolly here.' He drew out the thin folded wad that he kept in his deep back pocket and peeled off the notes. 'Here. Give her one for me.' William took the money without examining it and shambled off down the wharf side. 'See you tomorrow morning, early. We'll get her unloaded. Don't be late.' William turned, but that was all the acknowledgement that Ezra got.

He preferred being on the boat on his own, and when William had walked out of sight he sat in the corner of the stern and rolled himself a thin cigarette. The haunting notes of a melodeon drifted from among the moored barges. It came from a gaily painted Number One down the wharf. Ezra could see the man in the stern squeezing out the notes as his wife, dressed in her traditional black, washed their supper things at his side.

The noise of the loading and unloading of boats went on around him and the lights had begun to cast their glow more fully against the rapidly darkening sky. He felt a calm, just as on the night that he had walked from his whore's house in Silas Square to the Belle Vue those few weeks ago, the night before he had murdered a man.

Clouds were gathering. It was going to rain. His eyes caught the windlass on the shelf beneath the rudder. He had wiped it a thousand times in the last few weeks, but he reached out for it again and rubbed a greasy rag up and down its length. He dropped into his canvas bag his one or two shore clothes: a pair of trousers, a shirt and waistcoat, and took one last look around the cabin. It was just possible, he thought, that his next visit to his boat would be in the company of the police. It was all right, he had checked it a hundred times. He shut the little double doors and drew the locking plate over them. This he padlocked and then

did the same at the other end of the hatch. With his bag
over his shoulder, he began the two-mile walk to the
whore's house in Lozells.

Little Mary felt sorry for her mother. She looked like an old
woman. She never ate. The customers hadn't seen her for
weeks. Clifford wasn't admitted to her room. When he had
made her food and taken it to her, she wouldn't open the
door. He had whispered to her that it was outside. 'Please
eat something, Gertie. Let me see you. Let me talk to you.
Will you let me send for the doctor?' She said no to everything. He was afraid to force the issue, for he knew by now
that she must guess that he was involved, and in her state
of mind she couldn't be trusted not to blurt everything out,
compromise herself and implicate him. He had hoped that
her distress would lessen as the days passed. But she had
become worse.

As well as sympathy for her, he felt a deep resentment at
the strength of her feelings. This pricked him and made
him glad of the ill that he had done to his rival.

The food lay untouched on the tray. As Mary walked
down the landing she walked around it in a big arc, fearing
it as a symbol of all that was festering in this strange house-
hold which had changed so much in the last few weeks.

The *Birmingham Mail* revealed the murder on its front
page the day after the visit to the Belle Vue of the Inspector
and his sergeant. There was a photograph of the dead man,
taken some time ago, but clearly recognizable. The story
carried certain gruesome details of the crime and some wild
speculation as to the killer's motives. Clifford made certain
that the paper stayed downstairs in the bar where Gertrude
and Mary would not see it, but the following day, playing
with her friend Victoria, Mary had been shown it.

'The man who's been killed was a customer at your hotel,
it says,' Victoria burst out when they were down the

garden, the newspaper concealed beneath her cardigan. 'It says that the last time he was seen he was at your hotel. Isn't it awful?'

Mary's eyes grew wide in horror and amazement as she saw the hazy photograph of her friend Mr Beech.

'He's been killed? Mr Beech? But I knew him. He was my friend. He talked to me from the yard. And he gave me sixpence towards my farm.'

She had never understood the nature of the relationship between her mother and Beech, but she knew that it was, in some way, an inappropriate one. She had only to observe the contrast between her mother's and her father's behaviour on those afternoons when her mother swept past them out to the waiting Beech. This was not right. It couldn't be. But she said nothing to Victoria. She was embarrassed for both her mother and her father. She was also, unaccountably, ashamed for herself.

CHAPTER 18

The next morning Hammond picked up the sergeant at Steelhouse Lane police station and they drove in silence through the morning city traffic, up Colmore Row, through Paradise Street, down Broad Street and across Five Ways to the hotel on Icknield Port Road. The sergeant knew his boss well enough to know when to keep quiet. This was one of those times.

Although neither man voiced it, through throbbing heads and the noisy morning traffic, last night's prospect of progress through an unidentified quiet stranger looked woefully thin. Perhaps the landlord could throw some light on him. It was worth a try. But he would surely have mentioned the man if he had thought there was anything odd about him. Still, they might as well see. His wife, after all, had been ill. Maybe he had forgotten to say anything.

It was not yet opening time. They sat in the black Austin in silence and the Inspector lit his first Capstan.

There was the bang of a door shutting inside the backyard and then the great green double doors opened a crack and the child Mary slid out.

He wound down the window: 'Mary!' She looked at the two men squashed into their serious-looking car. 'It's all right dear, it's me, the policeman. We met when I was talking to your father on Saturday, do you remember?' She took a wary step towards the car, and then, recognizing him, she looked with questioning suspicion at the other man seated beside him. 'This is my sergeant. Say hello, Preston.'

'Hello, dear,' said the sergeant, leaning forward to show himself to her across the Inspector.

'My mummy said I'm not to talk to strangers. Not to anyone I don't know.'

'I'm very glad to hear it. It's the best advice your mummy could give you. But I'm not actually a stranger, am I? I think your mummy meant people you don't know at all. People who might harm you. Are you off to school?' he asked in a breezy manner.

'Yes,' she replied.

'Would you like to drive to school in my car?'

Yes,' she replied.

He waited but she made no move towards the door. 'Come on then, you'll be late.'

'I can't,' she said.

'Why not?' asked the Inspector.

'I have to meet my friend on the corner. I meet her every day.'

'We'll take you to the corner then, all right?' He pulled up the handle and she stepped into the back seat and sat right in the middle. 'Preston,' said the Inspector, and the car pulled away from the kerb.

'I'm a bit stuck on some things that I'm trying to find out, Mary. I wondered if you could help me at all?'

She said nothing but sat with the palms of her hands pressed gently down on either side of her in the middle of the brown-leather seat.

'Which corner is it that you're going to, Mary?' asked the sergeant.

'We're going in the wrong direction,' said the little girl. 'It's the other way.'

Preston looked at the Inspector and then at the little girl in the driving mirror, but there was no hint of mischievousness.

The sergeant turned the corner and headed back to where they had come from. The Inspector continued to lean back over his seat. 'Did you know Mr Beech, the man who died, Mary?'

Mary looked down at her shoes. Her feet didn't reach the floor of the car. 'Yes,' she said.

'How did you know him?' asked the Inspector.

'He was my friend,' said Mary. 'He used to talk to me on his way to . . . on his way through the backyard.'

'Were you in the backyard at that time of night?' asked the Inspector. He knew it didn't make sense. Although he hadn't even yet met her mother, the landlord's attitude to his daughter told him enough to know that they wouldn't let their daughter be in the vicinity of drinking men and the gents' urinal at night-time.

'Of course not, silly,' she said.

He didn't mind the friendly abuse, the intimacy that it signalled was much more important to him.

'I was up in my room. But Mr Beech was my friend. He always looked up. He talked to me. But we had to be quiet. Mummy and Daddy didn't know. I would have been in trouble. I think Mr Beech would have been in trouble too.'

The car had stopped. The sergeant had pulled up on the corner where a little girl stood with her hands folded in front of her, a school bag hung there.

'There's Irene,' said Mary, and she tapped on the window. The other girl looked up in amazement.

'Mary, just before you go to school, tell me: when did you last see Mr Beech? Think ever so hard because it's really important. Can you think of anything that will help you remember what day it was, what day of the week, what time, anything?'

'I know exactly,' said the little girl as she gently bounced up and down on the seat, her actions contrasting with the mounting sense of anticipation in the Inspector. 'It was the night that he threw me sixpence. I needed four-and-eleven for my farm. When he gave me sixpence, I only needed that week's pocket money from Daddy and I had enough. You can see my farm if you come to the house again.'

It was the first time that anyone in the family had ever called the hotel anything as intimate as a house.

'Thank you,' he said politely. 'And what day of the week was that?'

'It was on the Tuesday night. I have to go to school now. Irene will go without me.'

The other little girl was getting fed up with waiting. Mary could be a show-off and she was being one now. Jumping up and down on the back seat of a car with two old men in the front, what did she think she was doing? Irene would count to ten, and then she would go.

By the time she got to seven she began counting in halves. At eight and a half she taxed herself and went into quarters and counted very slowly. The man in the car was still talking and Mary was still answering, but now she was looking down at the floor. Irene got to ten and started to shuffle her feet.

'I must go to school. I'll be late and get into trouble,' said Mary.

'It was definitely a Tuesday evening, Mary?' said the Inspector.

'Yes.'

'Do you have any idea of the time?' probed the Inspector.

'It was dark, nearly dark anyway.'

'Four weeks ago, nearly dark, first week of September. What would that be? About half past nine or ten o'clock do you think, Mary?'

'Yes. I remember it was nearly dark because I couldn't see who it was, but I knew anyway.'

The Inspector sighed deeply. 'You said you knew who it was 'cause he'd thrown you a sixpence, you just said so.'

She was frightened by the change in his voice, the nasty, short tone.

'I don't mean him. Not Mr Beech. I mean the other one.
I couldn't see him, but I knew his walk. I'd heard him lots
of times. But he only came every so often. He was there,
then he'd go away.'

'For how long,' interrupted the Inspector. 'For two or
three weeks?'

'Yes. I suppose so. I'm not really sure.'

'And do you know who he was. What his name was?'

'No. He never spoke to me. He never looked up. But he
dragged one of his boots. I could tell his noise. He had an
iron thing on one of his boots and it made a special sort of
noise. And when he and Mr Beech had finished talking
outside the . . .'

'Yes, outside the Gents.'

'Then he went back first. Then Mr Beech stopped and
talked to me and threw me sixpence.'

Irene walked towards the car. She looked annoyed. She
had reached ten, and ten again, and done it in quarters
every one this time. She wanted to go but was now so late
that she was afraid to go alone. But most of all she wanted
to know what the mystery of Mary and the men in the car
was.

Mary put her hand on the handle and the Inspector
reached into his trouser pocket. He gave her a shilling and
said, 'You're a good girl, Mary Benyon. Buy yourself a
tractor for your farm on Saturday. Perhaps I'll come up
and have a look at it. Or even Preston here. He likes farms,
eh Sergeant?'

She got out and pushed the door to. He called after her,
'And tell your teacher that you had to speak to Inspector
Hammond. Tell her it was important. Goodbye. Good
girl.'

Two men observed standing together on a dark night in
September would not convict anyone of murder, but at least
a possible suspect had been seen speaking to the victim.

Things were improving. A little crack had appeared on the sheer cliff face and that crack might provide the finger-hold that the Inspector had been looking for.

CHAPTER 19

That evening a policeman sat in a window-seat at the Belle Vue looking straight ahead. He had half a pint of dark mild on the table, set square before him. He was in civilian clothes, but was obviously a policeman. Clifford knew who he was, the others who had been questioned knew who he was. And the young constable, with his fair moustache and jutting chin, knew that they knew.

Upstairs, stretched full-length on Mary's bedroom floor, surrounded by farm toys but at this moment playing snap with the seven-year-old, was Sergeant Preston. He was losing.

The sash window was open a few inches, and every time that he heard the door bang to as someone left the pub to cross the yard to the Gents, he eased himself up on his elbows and looked out from the gap between the curtains and down to the yard below.

Mary joined in this little game that they were playing, but each time she shook her head or said, 'No, silly. I'll tell you if he comes. I'll hear him. I'll know when I hear him.'

Clifford had had no choice but to co-operate in this exercise. The Inspector had told him how helpful little Mary had been to them that morning and that they wanted to follow up the possibility of a lead. The landlord told them that he thought he might vaguely remember the man that they were looking for. But it was difficult. One saw so many customers, week in and week out. Of course, the Inspector had said. Of course.

To have refused to help would only have drawn attention to himself. He merely asked that they should not keep Mary

awake longer than was absolutely necessary, and that they
certainly should not disturb his wife, who was still unwell
in her room.

Downstairs in the bar, as the doors swung open at the
arrival of every new customer, the policeman looked that
way. Clifford glanced up and returned to his pulling of pints
or ringing up the till. He tried to perform all these normal
functions with as much unself-consciousness as possible,
but he had become painfully aware of how very difficult it
was to do the most natural thing in the world when it took
place beneath the gaze of another's watchful eye.

The hint of autumn that the Newport sergeant had
smelled in his garden over a week ago had now been confirmed with the first early ground frost, and the saloon bar
doors were closed against the evening cool even though the
days were fine and clear. The leaves had started to turn,
the ash curling and browning at the edges, the occasional
chestnut falling before its time and rattling through the big
branches before bouncing into the gutter on the wide streets
of Edgbaston.

It was after nine-thirty and the saloon had developed
that entity which grows when several men have drunk two
or three pints of beer and the light has gone outside and
they are drawn together beneath the lamps within and the
fire at the far end throbs a life of its own. This was the good
time in every pub's inner life.

The door opened and Talbot walked in. He didn't look
aside. He registered nothing.

'Good evening. What can I get you?' said the landlord.

'Whisky and water, and a half of bitter.' There was nothing in the reply. Whatever had gone wrong that had led to
the discovery of the body must have been beyond Ezra's
control. If he knew he was in a corner, he was going to walk
straight out of it. They could stand and watch, but he'd give
them nothing. Clifford admired his graceless composure.

The policeman knew this was his man. He had a vague description. It fitted.

'One and nine, please.' Ezra handed him a ten-shilling note, and held his hand steady and straight out as Clifford fingered up the change from the deep drawers in the great silver-plated National Cash Register.

'Thank you,' he said, and walked to his usual seat in the corner. He drank the whisky down and sipped at the beer. The smoke-room was quieter than usual. The landlord's wife was nowhere to be seen. It all made sense. He rolled himself a cigarette and kept his eyes towards the floor.

After his second beer he got up and walked to the door that led to the yard. Even before the big policeman had got to his elbows the little girl was at the curtains. 'That's him,' she said. 'That's the man, listen.' The policeman looked through the tiny gap in the curtains and saw the man with his slight limp and heavy gait. At every other step there was a slight drag to his boot and the scrape of some sort of metal on its heel. He glowed a smile at the little girl and gently drew her back from the window.

As Talbot walked back across the yard he flicked his eyes up to the bedrooms. Two lights on. The little girl's, no doubt. But the other one? The landlord's wife, perhaps. That's the danger, he thought. She's taken it badly and pulled away.

Talbot took his seat again and wondered what the next move was. Was Benyon in league with them? He drained his glass. Other customers were leaving.

'Good night, Clifford.'

'Good night, Jimmy. Good night, Sid.' Clifford cleared the glasses and wiped tables.

Ezra got to his feet and walked towards the door.

'Good night,' he muttered, but didn't wait for a reply.

He was aware of measured footsteps behind him. When

he had gone twenty yards a voice without ceremony said, 'Oy, you.'

Ezra turned to look at the face behind him.

'What d'you want?'

'We're from the police. We've got a few questions for you. Step this way, please.' It wasn't a request and the two men took a half-step closer to him, the speaker gesturing with his hand towards the car parked in darkness on the other side of the street. The window was open a few inches, blue smoke wafting out.

They walked to the car and got into the back seat. A policeman sat on either side of him. Ezra, the big man, squashed between the two smaller, younger men.

'Good evening,' said the voice of the Inspector from the front seat. He didn't turn around and Talbot craned his neck to see the speaker's face in the little driving mirror.

'What's all this about?' asked Ezra.

'I need to ask you a few questions, about an acquaintance of yours. I think we'd be more comfortable down at the station, don't you?' Again this was no question and as if to confirm it, the car pulled away from the pavement, juddering a little under the weight of its five occupants.

There could have been no greater contrast between the two men as they sat opposite each other in the bare interview room on the second floor. The Inspector had a pinkish bloom to his close-shaven cheeks, he exuded well-being and good health; his shirt was clean and starched, his tie sober, his dark suit recently pressed.

Ezra Talbot, the boatman seated before him, had spent the day on the wharf unloading bales of cotton and, later, loading the iron rods that he was to carry to Market Drayton tomorrow: although he had washed, his big strong hands were grimy and his cracked and broken nails carried half-moons of dirt.

The Inspector had decided to attack. 'A Mr Beech. You know the man I am referring to?' said the Inspector.

'Never heard of him,' replied Ezra. 'Why?'

'He's dead,' said the Inspector.

'So what? I've never heard of the bloke.'

'Are you certain?'

'Never heard of him. What's it to do with me anyway?'

'You couldn't oblige me with the answer to that question and save me a great deal of time and trouble, I suppose?' came the Inspector's answer, the words barely out of the bargeman's mouth.

The Inspector got up and walked across to the black window. 'You have nothing to say about motive, I suppose?' he said, while looking out into the night.

Talbot stared at his back, but said nothing. He had imagined some scenarios during the preceding days, but this certainly was not one of them. He had imagined being in a room and being questioned, possibly by several men. He certainly thought that he might be hit, but of that he had no fear. It would help him to resist. But what of this buffoon? This well-kept, well-polished, dandified fool? No wonder the world was full of thieves and murderers if this was the kind of bloke who was supposed to be out there catching them. The man was clearly insane. But his insanity had to be watched. Think first and speak carefully. They haven't got a thing on you, he told himself. They haven't got a thing.

'Shall we have a cup of tea, gentlemen?' asked the Inspector after peering out of the yellow-lit room into the black night outside. 'Would you care for a cup of tea, Mr Talbot?'

'Yes. I'll have some tea.'

The constable left the room.

'Where have you just come from, Mr Talbot?'

'From the Belle Vue—you just picked me up, remember?' quipped Ezra.

'Very good, Mr Talbot. I like a sense of humour. The only problem is, it does tend to delay things rather, and, while time isn't of the absolute essence, there is always so very much to do. Can we try again? Where have you just returned from, this trip?'

'I've been up North, to Cheshire. Why?'

'What were you carrying?'

'Coal.'

'Coal, to Cheshire? Don't they have their own coal up there? I thought they had plenty of coal in the North-West, or was I led astray at school?'

'It's a special coal they need. Midlands coal, for manufacturing.'

'Ah, thank you. I see now. You have a crew?'

'Of course.'

'How many?'

'One.'

'One. He walks the horse? You don't hire a drover for stages?'

'No. He walks the horse.'

'And what do you do when the boat requires both of you to be on board?'

'Like when?'

'Oh, tunnels and the like.'

'He walks the beast round and then we leg through. Same at locks. He walks her round, then we work through the flight.'

'So you have plenty of time alone?'

'Not nearly enough!'

'You don't care for your crew member, Mr Talbot, do I detect?'

'I like my own company best. He gets on. I get on. There's no need for a lot of chat.'

'And where does he spend the night, this man—what's his name, by the way, your employee?'

'William.'

'William. William what?'

'William . . . I don't know. I've never asked him.'

'I see. And where does William sleep?'

'On board.'

'Always?'

'Usually.'

'When does he not sleep on board?'

'When we're back here for a day or two.'

'I see. Then you stay on board, but he goes . . . ?'

'I dunno where he goes.'

'Come, come, Mr Talbot, where does William what-ever-'is-name-is go when you are tied up in Birmingham?'

'He goes and gets a woman, I think.'

'The same woman?'

'How should I know? I don't give a damn what he does. Just so long as he walks the horse and opens the locks I don't give a damn.'

'So you stay on board alone?'

'Sometimes. When we're tied up here.'

The constable shouldered open the door and brought in the tea. The Inspector ignored him and went back to the window, where he again stood very close to the glass and peered out into the complete blackness. Ezra couldn't tell, but it seemed that it was either a yard or a brick wall out there. There was no light and no movement. The Inspector gazed out intently. Ezra took the spilt tea from the saucer and poured it into his cup.

'You must have been very surprised to hear about the body?'

'What are you on about? I don't know anything about any body.'

'Of course, we're still pretending; I'd forgotten for a moment. I'll tell you what you're not supposed to know. In the interests of brevity.'

'In the interests of who?'

'The body was found very quickly, a happy accident, a little girl, a cuff-link . . .'

Ezra felt the tear, felt the catch of the sacking on something as he pulled the corpse along the towpath. That blasted mooring spike had been his undoing.

'Some good detective work from a sharp-eyed officer out where you dropped the body in. He connected the initials on the link and the name on the missing person poster in his station. But you must have been surprised.' He turned round sharply. 'Are you still pretending that you don't know anything about this? That's rather unlikely isn't it? It's been in the papers. News travels down the waterways as well as everywhere else, doesn't it?'

'If it's the bloke who was pulled out at Cowley, I did hear about that, everybody has. There aren't that many people pulled out of the cut dead, are there?'

The Inspector gave no answer. He looked steadily at Ezra. 'So, you killed him here in Birmingham, at the wharf. You hid the body, or even dragged it underwater behind the barge. I thought about that, but I think it'd be a bit risky, wouldn't it? It might be seen, or it could catch on something, or come adrift and be lost before you'd hidden it and weighted it. All sorts of problems there, I think. No, I think hidden on board. Load of coal, hidden among that. You have a sheet over cargo of that sort? A little temporary resting place for the . . . the deceased.'

Ezra felt extremely ill at ease. Although this was plain common sense and the Inspector had said nothing that could not have been guessed at if he thought that the boatman was the killer, to have the crime outlined in this way was frightening in its accuracy.

'And then, of course, a good few miles from the scene of the crime, at one of the opportunities presented to you by the absence of . . . William, is it? While he is walking the horse around the tunnel, you drop the body in. I like it. It has a nice simplicity to it. It shouldn't have been discovered for years. That stretch has only recently been dredged, it's good and deep. Well-built too, shouldn't be any danger of a breach there, busy commercial thoroughfare. When did you dump the body, night or morning?'

There was no answer from Ezra. The Inspector walked to the table and dipped the tip of his index finger into his cup of tea. It was cold.

'Did you moor there?'

'Where?'

'At Cowley Tunnel?'

'No.'

'Where did you moor close to the tunnel?'

'We moored where we always do on that route. At Church Eaton. Lots of us do. There's good stabling and a pub.'

'Yes. And an hour or two away from the tunnel entrance the next morning.'

Ezra began to roll a cigarette and the Inspector lit another of his Capstans. He held the burning match to Talbot's face before the man had finished rolling his cigarette. The boatman hastily licked the gum and put the cigarette between his lips. But the Inspector let the match fall to the floor and returned to the window.

'What had Beech done to you?'

'I don't know who you're talking about. I've never met the man.'

'He drank in the Belle Vue. You must have known him.'

'Lots of people drink in the Belle Vue. I don't know them. I don't know anybody in there. I just go in there for a quiet drink.'

'Do you think he was queer, Talbot?'

'How should I know?'

'Well, not to be over-delicate, sometimes queers try and

pick up the wrong people, and those people get annoyed. Are you queer, Talbot?'

'What are you on about? I'm a boatman. Of course I'm not bloody queer. You wouldn't last long out there if you were.'

'Yes. Do you think he was, though?' And before he had time to answer! 'I know he had women friends, but a lot of men, so I'm told, they . . . you know, both, men and women. Strikes me as a bit odd, too, but apparently it goes on. What were your impressions of him?'

'Look, I don't have any impressions 'cause I never knew him. If he drank in the Belle Vue, I might have seen him. But I never knew him, I never saw him as far as I know.'

'You must've heard him. He played the piano, sang a bit too. Yorkshireman. Everybody liked him . . .'

'Somebody didn't,' said Ezra.

'Yes, you're right, Mr Talbot. But why not? Why not, I wonder?'

Ezra wouldn't budge. The Inspector was delighted that the man claimed he had never met Beech. Given little Mary's sighting of them, it only confirmed his strong intuition that the boatman was involved. If he needed more, it came shortly when Talbot revealed to him that he did a bit of illegal buying and selling, fencing stolen property from up North and selling it in the Midlands, vice-versa sometimes if there was any trade that way. People never told you these things unless they were 'trading'. Talbot was hoping that the Inspector would think he was more plausible if he gave him a sop. Of course he did a bit of illegal dealing. Who didn't? But involvement with a murder? Certainly not.

The Inspector wasn't having any of it. He knew this was his man. But he didn't yet know why, and he didn't know how to prove it either. The word of a sensible seven-year-old had been a breakthrough. But you couldn't hang a case on it. Much less a man.

As he stood looking out into the blackness before him for minute after long minute, what he did know was that the continued non-appearance of Gertrude Benyon at her home and place of work was looking more and more suspicious. He didn't like it, and yet he did like it: the longer she didn't appear, the more inclined he was to think that there might be some connection between all these events: a man who drinks at the pub is murdered; another man who drinks at the same pub was seen to speak to him yet denies it; the landlord's wife becomes unwell and is not seen in public for weeks at just about the same time as these other things take place. The pieces might not be fitting together yet, but they were starting to appear.

'It's getting late, Mr Talbot. I have a home to go to. Do *you* have a home to go to?'

'The boat,' said Ezra, defensively.

'Do you have any . . . female company? Anyone that you visit regularly in Birmingham?'

'Who doesn't?'

'And who is she? Where does she live? I might need to have a word with her. Would you give the constable the details. I'm going home, but I think I'd like you to accept a bed here tonight. I might have some more questions for you tomorrow.'

Before Ezra could protest, the Inspector had made the nonsensical invitation into a non-negotiable statement.

'Yes. I will have some more questions for you. I'll see you tomorrow. Sleep well.'

CHAPTER 20

He said that he had to speak to her. He had to. There was something in his voice that she had never heard before and, even in her broken sorrow, she knew that she had to admit him. She got up from the bedside chair where she had been sitting all evening, her feet up on the bed, and with her dressing-gown open and falling about her, walked to the bedroom door.

He whispered again, 'Gertie. Gertie, can you hear me? I must speak to you. It's very important. We have to talk.'

She turned the key and pulled open the door.

The room had a bad smell and he was shocked at her appearance. She wore a slip beneath her dressing-gown, but where it hung open he could see her sagging breasts. He looked away, but she stood there defiantly, challenging him with her decrepitude.

'What do you think? Do you like what you see?' She didn't look down but his eyes were drawn up and down her, from her rounded shoulders to her protruding pelvic bone. His brown eyes pricked with tears. She was wasting away. Her white skin had a yellow tinge. Her hair was lank.

'Gertrude. We have to talk. Things are very bad, not only this—' he cast his eyes about the room—'but what's happening outside. Get dressed, please. Have a wash and let's talk.'

She looked at him and he felt that her indifference was lit by a flicker of interest in what he was saying. Yes, he did mean Beech, but he wasn't going to say his name. Not now. She took a deep breath of the stale air and turned away. There was lipstick and make-up smeared on the sheets; there were clothes strewn on the floor, underwear and winter coats, dresses and shoes. The dressing-table was covered in powder and there were big smudges on the mirror. The red Du Maurier cigarette packet was over-flowing with stubs. She had covered the bedside lamp with a headscarf. It looked dangerous to him. He had a fear of fire.

She walked to the dressing-table and stood in front of the mirror with her head bowed, the dressing-gown hanging open. He realized that she was waiting for him to go, to leave her alone.

'I'll make a pot of tea. Have a little wash. Come to the kitchen. We'll talk. Please.'

His tone was loving and concerned, but without owner-ship and possession. He drew the bedroom door to and heard the soft click of its catch. He was filled with love and sorrow for her.

She had drawn the brush through her dirty, greasy hair and it lay flat and lifeless, close to her skull. Her dark-brown eyes were deep in their sockets. She had drawn her dressing-gown to with the belt of a blue summer dress. Her feet were bare.

She stood at the open kitchen door and watched him. He put the tea-things on the table and drew up a chair for her. He pulled the other one round and sat at the pine table. She stayed by the open door and looked aimlessly about the kitchen, as if at any moment she might walk away from this business, her flicker of interest extinguished.

But she stayed. He gestured to the chair and she looked at it as if seeing it for the first time. When she sat, her palms flat on the table in front of her, he reached out and put his fingers on the back of her white hand.

'Will you have some tea, Gertie?'

She didn't answer and he poured her a cup, pushing it very carefully towards her.

Could she cope with the full story? Could she be trusted with it? He thought not. But if he didn't get to her, get through to her, the Inspector would, and God knew what would follow from that. 'It's about . . .' He still found difficulty saying the word, his mouth dried. He forced it slowly out. 'It's about Beech, Gertie.' He stopped. He had paired their names. Unintentionally, he had yoked them in this way, and for a moment the old loathing for what had been between these two was predominant again.

'You know something's happened to him? Do you know that, Gertie? Something dreadful's happened to him.' He was watching her closely. She knew. There was no surprise. And she knew he would tell her. She said nothing.

'The police have been here. Yesterday, and then again last evening. They spoke to Mary. She had seen something. That man Talbot. He was seen talking to Beech. I think they suspect he might be involved.' Did he imagine it, or was there the tiniest parting of the lips that suggested a knowing sneer?

'They'll question you, Gertie. They'll have to. I've told them you're ill, can't be seen, but they're getting suspicious. It's been over three weeks since you've been seen downstairs. "Why haven't you had the doctor? What's the matter with you?" That kind of thing. They'll want to talk to you . . . about Beech. And what you knew of him. You're— we're—going to have to decide. What we say will affect the way they . . . proceed. If they find . . .'

'Stop, Clifford.' He was shocked to hear her speak; wholly taken aback. 'I know what you're saying. Don't go on in this way.' She was lucid. She did understand. But did that mean that she would act sensibly? Sensibly for him?

There was a long silence and then: 'But was it necessary? Whatever you did?' She raised her watering eyes to him and said again, 'Did you have to do that thing?' Her continued look meant that she actually wanted him to answer.

Looking across at her brokenness, he felt that surely nothing was worth this. But he had done it. At the time he would have burned for her. He remembered that pain and met her eyes and said, 'Yes, I did. I couldn't go on.'

She held his face in her eyes. How rarely she had looked at him. She was seeing his face for the first time. The hairs that curled slightly round his ears, the lines near the corner of his eyes. She hadn't looked at him for years. She was shocked and ashamed. The hurt that she had done him had never really touched her. *She* had never been hurt in that way, and did not understand it. She wouldn't allow anyone to do to her what she had done to Clifford. She used to think: Why doesn't he take a woman? I would! The man has no mettle. No spine. She had held him in contempt. But now she understood something which she had never done before. They were looking deep into one another.

From her deep-set, dark-brown eyes a tear started to roll, full and slowly down her cheek and into the corner of her mouth. It rested there a moment before the next one eased it out and down to her chin. He watched them come and gather, and eventually the first one burst on to the table beneath her. She was weeping deeply, in her whole being. She pushed out her hand towards him and the tears fell on to it, and then, as Clifford laid his over it, they fell and bounced off him.

CHAPTER 21

It was the Inspector's wife's time of the month. They continued to share a bed, but there was a metaphorical wall down the centre of the mattress between them. He had a tendency to gravitate towards her ample softness during the night, and they would often wake with his legs coiled about her, his arms wrapped around her midriff and bosom. In this way, his erection would stir and they would begin to make nocturnal love. Although it was never discussed afterwards, they both knew that it was the best sexual loving that took place between them. Their natural inhibitions were in abeyance, he was relaxed from the pressures of his work, his inquiries and interrogations, his contemplation of robbers and corpses, his appearances in courts and at prisons. She was simply less embarrassed about the act taking place between them, the essential sinfulness of their dark pleasure. She would feign half-sleep long after she was awake to what was happening. It made the act more enjoyable for her, and it allowed the Inspector the freedom to mutter his lascivious thoughts as he moved up and down against her, admired her breasts, holding her, and then drew her to him. Bethan's little gasps of pleasure spurred him on and he spent himself into her with good abandon.

It was during these nocturnal trysts that they would frequently achieve mutual satisfaction. Afterwards, they would lie there, he crooked in her arm, a risible sight, his six-foot frame bent to her warm body against him, her arm about his shoulder. He loved her.

At this time of the month, though, he needed to be aware. She wore clothes about her protection and lay far from him in the wide bed that had come with her at the time of their marriage, come in a motor van from her family home in Newtown, Montgomeryshire, to the big house in Thornhill Road in Handsworth.

He lay on his back and listened to her deep, steady breathing. She was asleep. His hands were folded absurdly behind his head on the pillow. He was wide awake and his mind was active. Between the crack in the bedroom curtains, he could see the reason for his wakefulness: the full moon. There was plenty of evidence of its awesome power in the prisons and mental hospitals of the country, evidence there of the people who were affected by this force that could swing the ocean's tides and make men kill for sixpence or an argument over who won the Cup Final in 1927; people who would be rational at other times of the month, yet for whom this period of the lunar cycle was stimulating to their own particular lunacy.

But over the years the Inspector had learned to try and manage and exploit this phenomenon in himself. He knew himself well enough to know that it was no myth that the moon affected people's behaviour; certainly it affected his. He knew that he had tremendous energy at these times, but he was also very sensitive, easily offended, susceptible to arguments with his wife or colleagues or recalcitrant taxi-drivers. It was as if all his nerve-endings were exposed. He could feel well, and feel much, but pain and angst also found easy access to him.

He was not a particularly clever man, but he was usually sensitive and observant. However, during the period of this subtle but important change in his behaviour every month, he had learned certain subjects—the missing sock, the newspaper not folded, or not to comment on the fact that it was cauliflower cheese for supper: he really didn't like cauliflower cheese. He tried to let it pass, but not always entirely successfully. In spite of himself, he would say something, the least thing, and then . . . Was it him, or was the normally placid Bethan over-reacting to his little criticism?

In retrospect, as they occupied different parts of the house for the rest of the evening and he perhaps walked down to the local pub and stood at the bar for an hour with a whisky and soda in front of him, he would reflect that perhaps it had been foolish of him to say anything, knowing how prone he was at this time of the month to take offence.

But he always allowed himself a little qualification: if she knew that he was obsessive about a neatly folded newspaper, and if she knew that he abhorred cauliflower cheses, then why on earth did she leave the paper crumpled and make the detested dish? And particularly at this time?

Although taking offence and petty argument came easily and he had learned to beware of them, if not totally to avoid them, he also had an inordinate amount of energy at this period. He would rise early, work long and purposefully, come up with some crucial fact on an inquiry or perform quite perfunctory tasks quickly and efficiently; reports would get written, people seen, things filed that had been cluttering his desk and office. At home, routine, mechanical tasks would be undertaken efficiently, and with whistling, high spirits. He would hum his favourite arias as he cleaned all the family's shoes in one session. Even those that were clean would get another polish and shine. He was fulfilled, singing on the cellar steps as he sat there on a sheet of newspaper, sleeves rolled up, and surrounded by half a dozen pairs of shoes of all shapes and sizes. He would think himself happy until, emerging from the cellar, Bethan would ask him why he needed to clean shoes in his best shirt which was now smudged with Cherry Blossom boot polish. From this peak of simple happiness, he would be crestfallen.

The wind blew out from the holes rent in his sails. He would have no appetite for an argument and would saunter into the garden to amble in the vegetable patch, pulling a weed here, breaking off a blackfly-ridden beantop there and feeling generally fed up and affronted like a fractious schoolboy.

And so it was their time of the month. Bethan lay there quietly, pulsing her menstrual blood into her sanitary towels and thick underpants, breathing deeply and contentedly, and John Hammond lay wide awake, his hands clasped tightly behind his head on the pillow, his mind racing through the case before him.

He became aware of just how tightly his fingers were knotted into one another and relaxed them, but within two or three minutes, as he followed his thoughts again, they were tense once more.

Talbot was not going to budge. He knew his ground, and he knew as well as the Inspector did that there was no chance of his story being exposed unless there was a breakthrough from some other source. The Inspector was keeping to himself Mary's sighting of Talbot and Beech. Confronted with this piece of information, Talbot could blankly say, 'So what?' He would know as well as anyone that it could not convict him of any crime. No, the Inspector would hold that little nugget for future use, when it could be really made to pay.

No one had seen anything from the bridge near where the body had been found, they'd already interviewed half the villagers of Gnosall and Church Eaton. The few people who had been around at that time had seen nothing at all unusual.

This hired hand, this man William though, he might know something of the crime, and he might be an easier target. They would pick him up tomorrow and try and break him down. If he wasn't involved—and the Inspector rather doubted it, for Talbot was the self-sufficient, loner type, not the sort to jeopardize a scheme by involving others unless it were absolutely necessary—then they might be able to get something out of him. Had he noticed anything unusual or odd about Talbot's behaviour in recent weeks?

But the person who was going to have to be interviewed was the elusive Gertrude Benyon. Her non-appearance had always looked suspicious, but when, only a day after the Inspector had spent the evening in the Belle Vue with his sergeant and spoken to the regulars, a short note, written in an educated hand and on good quality writing paper, had arrived on his desk at police headquarters, it became overwhelmingly so.

There was none of the petty criminal's or malicious gossip's attempts to conceal the sender's identity. It was not signed, or so the Inspector conjectured, simply because to have done so would embarrass the sender. But the assured copperplate writing could easily be traced, should the need arise. And the author knew this as well as anyone. But it didn't matter. It was quite immaterial which of the small group of regulars in the smoke-room had put black ink on good paper and written, '*You should know, Inspector, that Mrs Benyon and Mr Beech were* very *good friends.*' This was all the Inspector needed to give him the impetus to break down the flimsy defences which her husband kept trying to place in his way.

The Inspector could hardly wait for tomorrow. He would start to prise and uncover. If only he could start now.

The moon's light was ample for him to read the time on the Hunter by his bedside. It was twenty-five minutes to three. It was going to be a very long night. He unclenched his fingers again and closed his eyes. But even beneath the closed lids, the images flashed, the faces, the questions, the interviews, the way he would trick the truth out of them. He knew all the ruses. He would tie them in knots.

His fingers were clenched again. He unlocked them, turned on his side away from his wife and, with one hand under his head, tried to sleep.

CHAPTER 22

She was a handsome woman. There had been something seriously wrong with her, probably still was, he thought, but she had a sombre beauty in spite of her emaciation. He thought of his own wife. They must be very similar in age. Their children, both daughters, were only a year or so apart. What does a man do if his wife dies at this age? Dies and leaves him to bring up a girl of seven or eight or nine? It didn't bear thinking about, but every time that he looked across the kitchen table at her, he thought of her mortality, her beauty, and of his own wife's mortality and her blooming health.

She had bathed and dressed in a dark morning dress that accentuated her pale, thin face and dark-brown eyes. She offered the Inspector coffee and made it for them as he spoke. She was very composed. She had not yet emerged from that self-imposed silence of the last three weeks and she felt a sense of calm compounded of the grief, distress and isolation within her. Not feeling of this world, she felt this world held no terror for her. She knew that this man could not reach her, not frighten her, no matter what his suggestions or implications were going to be.

She put the willow-pattern coffee cups, milk and sugar on the table between them, and then the steaming, aromatic coffee. Then she folded her hands on the table, on the spot where last night's tears had fallen and where she had known that she was going to stay with Clifford and be his wife again.

Her very serenity disadvantaged the Inspector. The schemes that had flooded through his over-active mind as he had lain awake in bed last night now evaporated at the sight and presence of her. Perhaps it was that very over-activity and lack of sleep that was making him feel less than incisive as he sat opposite this frail and beautiful woman.

'You must know, Mrs Benyon, that we are investigating the death of one of your customers, someone whom I believe was known to you personally?'

'My husband has told me, yes.' She did not look up. 'I was naturally very sorry to hear of it. He was more than a customer, he was a friend.'

'Of course,' said the Inspector. He was taking his tone from her, becoming almost reverential. 'You say he was a friend. Could you tell me a little more about him?' The anonymous note in its thick cream envelope was in his jacket pocket. He felt like a general in possession of the luxury of a spare battalion on the battlefield.

'He was known to both Clifford and me as a good customer, but also a gentleman, a courteous and polite man who was popular with the other customers in the hotel.' There was no self-consciousness about her use of the word hotel. Was her punctiliousness about this word indicative also of her rather formal choice of words to describe Beech? She called him a friend but then gave a litany of adjectives that came from a catalogue or a book, 'polite, courteous, a gentleman, popular with the other customers'. These were not the words that described actual friendship, but rather the notion of it.

'Did your friendship extend any further than in the hotel, Mrs Benyon?' The question was intended to be open-ended, allowing offence if it were seen there. 'Did Mr Beech see you socially, apart from on licensed premises?' The 'you' could be singular or plural.

'We never received Mr Beech upstairs or out of hours, but he always inquired after our daughter. He was a traveller in surgical goods, you must know, I'm sure; and he took me out in his car occasionally. We don't own a car, Inspector. Would you like more coffee?'

He pushed his cup across the table. She was developing a degree of animation. It was only slight, but she was starting to emerge from her protective chrysalis.

He decided to prise a little. 'I am sure that any questions relating to this matter must be very difficult for you, Mrs Benyon, especially given your recent ill health, but I'm sure that you do see that I have to ask them?'

'Of course, Inspector. I understand.'

'It is particularly difficult when they are questions of a personal nature; you do see, don't you, Mrs Benyon?'

'I'm sure you only do what you feel you have to do, Inspector.'

Did he detect a slight threat to him not to pursue her any more assiduously than was absolutely necessary?

'A man has been murdered, Mrs Benyon. We have a body. We do not have a motive. We do not have a murderer. If we can find the former, I am sure that the latter will follow. Do you see?'

'I am sure that that is the way of police work, Inspector.'

'Quite.' She was starting to hedge a little, he felt certain. 'You went out "occasionally" with Mr Beech in his car, you say? Your husband accompanied you on these trips?'

'No. My husband doesn't care for motoring. He never has done. I enjoy it greatly.'

'And where did you drive to alone with Mr Beech?' The intention was to wound and she felt it.

'We drove to the countryside, to the Lickey hills sometimes, to Birmingham if I needed to shop. It was very kind of him, it's not easy to travel by tram always, or bus, especially the hours that have to be worked in a hotel.'

'Of course,' said the Inspector. 'And your husband? I'm sorry to ask these things of you, Mrs Benyon, but your

husband, did he not object to you accompanying Mr Beech
on jaunts in his car alone?'

He had drawn another arrow from his quiver and it, too,
hit home. It was important that he should, he had no idea
how many weapons were in there, nor how long he would
have with this woman before she claimed her illness was
too incapacitating for her to go on.

She took the arrow and snapped it cleanly in two. 'There
were no "jaunts", Inspector. There were a few motor trips
on which my husband did not wish to come. There was no
resentment on his part, of that I can assure you. I'm sure
you have spoken to him. But I don't see my husband as a
murderer anyway.' She looked up at him, her eyes defiant
and challenging. 'Do you?'

She was becoming confident. She was taunting him. And
she had mettle, notwithstanding her illness. But no man
approved of his wife going out with another man. Or at
least no man that the Inspector had ever met, and that was
good enough for him.

Did she know about the suspect, he wondered? Had her
husband told her that they had been awaiting his return,
and had arrested him? He decided not to mention it. He
had got enough. He would go and do a little prising on
Talbot. He would keep the hard-won initiative and leave
before she asked him to. These things were a battle. Sometimes bloody war, sometimes cagey chess. But always someone was slightly ahead, someone was in the better position.
He would leave now and consolidate that slight advantage.
'I think that will be all for now, Mrs Benyon. I can see that
you have not been at your best and I don't want to tire
you.'

'I can cope, Inspector. If there is anything else, please
stay and ask me.' She was clutching at the straw of avoiding
further questioning. Let's get it over with, her rational plea
was saying. Sometimes it was good to pursue when the

suspect felt like this. In their desire to get it over with, they would become confused, tire, make mistakes, and leave that little crack into which the Inspector would push the sharp point of his experience, and then he would twist and push and flex, and at every moment a little more light would enter the crevice, and eventually the darkness of the crime would be exposed to the light of his inquiring mind. It had an apocalyptic ring. He recognized this. But he didn't mind. He saw it in exactly these terms.

But this was not one of those times. He didn't have enough to go on yet. Now was a time to leave, with the battle not won, but with the high ground temporarily secured. A time to amble in the garden. Perhaps a time to lie awake at night, fingers knotted and the mind racing, but leaving the enemy also to think, leaving them in their beds and at their pillows, to weaken and to start to fall. Until, like the autumn fruit, when the moment was ready, into your hands they would drop.

'I really think that that will do for today, Mrs Benyon. Thank you again, and I do wish you a speedy recovery. Good day, ma'am.'

When Gertrude outlined the nature of the Inspector's questioning to Clifford in the kitchen after closing time that afternoon, they both knew he had decided that the most fruitful line of inquiry had to be the connection between herself and Beech. They even wondered if he imagined that the relationship between herself and Beech had soured— perhaps another woman—and that *she* had been involved in the murder. Without any direct accusation from him, it was difficult to tell where his suspicions lay.

But Clifford was only too aware that it was just a short step, as short as the one over the empty pit of the gaping gallows, to the link between himself and Beech. The house of cards would fall. Motive. Murderer. The Inspector would push until he got there. One of them would fall, be made to trip and stumble and begin the careering down the scree that would end in execution. All the connections, although only tenuously made, were there. How long would it be before this persistent policeman started to bring the threads together?

He had an option, thought Clifford. He had to proceed with caution; he was frankly unsure of the degree of Gertie's commitment to him. She could, after all, suddenly turn: find herself as filled with disgust and hatred for the perpetrators of this crime as she had been until yesterday. It was unlikely, Clifford thought, for the change that he felt he was witnessing in her was a sea-change.

He would implicate Talbot. At the right moment he would lead the Inspector to him, the plausible killer, and away from himself.

Mary sidled into the kitchen and stood at her father's side. This was the first time that she had seen her parents talking or sitting together for ages. She was glad. But she also hoped that her father would still be as nice and kind to her as he had been since her mother's illness.

They had established certain routines. She now brought his coffee to the bar each weekend morning. He gave her sixpence, a silver sixpence, on Saturdays, and he had even got down among the people and the animals of her new farm and mooed and played and moved the pieces at her behest. It wasn't quite right, of course, having someone else do these things with you—they never made quite the right noise or moved the farmer in quite the right way—but it was very fine to have her father in with her to share her pleasure, even if his breath did smell rather of warm whisky and his eyes started to drop after a few minutes of farmyard games.

CHAPTER 23

William sauntered along Nechells Wharf in the half-light
of the early October dawn and kicked a stump of wood
before him. Only one of his boots was laced, and that with
a piece of string. The other had broken days ago and since
then he had simply flexed his toes at each step to keep it
on. Smoke was slowly rising from several of the boats tied
up alongside the wharf.

Crow was empty, William knew that before he got there.
It was like an empty house. You could tell by the knock on
the door. You could tell with a boat by looking at it.

'Let's go aboard,' said the plain-clothes policeman from
behind him. William stood in wonder as the man undid the
padlock and pushed back the hatch-cover.

Sitting in the cabin, the policeman told William nothing,
but asked him everything he knew about his employer: his
whereabouts, his behaviour, his habits.

William was less help than could have been expected.
His slow delivery and gaping mouth were no affectation.
The man was genuinely dim-witted. He had noticed nothing unusual about Talbot. Hadn't spoken to him for days,
other than responding to instructions to go ahead with the
horse, open the lock, go and get some sugar, put on some
tea.

Yes, they had gone through Autherley at Wolverhampton, then up to Church Eaton and Cowley, they always did
if they were going that route. Yes, William had been off
the boat when they were last tied up at Birmingham in
Nechells. He always was. Anyway, William was a man,
liked to go and get some—you know. Yes. The plain-clothes
sergeant did know.

The sergeant knew that the Inspector hadn't held out much hope, but this was less than nothing.

The sergeant locked the hatch and slipped away the key. No, he couldn't tell William when Talbot would be back. William stood there looking at the greasy cut. He didn't know whether to be pleased at not working or displeased at no pay. Whether to be glad that his employer was obviously in some sort of trouble, or annoyed at the prospect of not having a job. He kicked a half brick into the water and cursed his way down the wharf.

The Inspector stood over the brown tops of his potato plants, the garden fork in his hand. It was a good crop and free of blight. As he lifted the nests of smooth, cream pebbles he brushed the earth from them and dropped them into a pile at his feet. The haulms he gathered and carried to his bonfire. He ran the fork through the hole where the plants had been and forked over the weed-free and lifeless soil. Potatoes cleaned the garden wonderfully well, but they also left it barren.

Emily joined him and picked up some of the potatoes, 'Did you grow these, Daddy?'

He was still proud of everything that he grew. 'I did, my lovely. They're good, aren't they? Your daddy's a good gardener.'

'Shall I take some in to Mummy?'

'Yes, darling, she's waiting for them.'

She carried a basketful away and he stood there, savouring the October morning.

Later, he sat at the kitchen table and peeled the potatoes in a large enamel basin. Bethan stood at the other end and forced stuffing into the chicken.

He knew the inquiry was at that difficult stage where the breakthrough was close yet elusive. Talbot was still in custody; William, his hand, had thrown no light on matters concerning his employer or the killing. The Inspector did not wish to return to the Belle Vue until he had something new, something with which to force either Benyon or his wife's hand.

He could attack them directly, confront them with the anonymous note perhaps, but this course had its pitfalls. They would no longer have to retain the pretence of innocence; they would become entrenched and defensive under the accusation of guilt. This could well prove counter-productive. He had seen it before. At the moment, they were all maintaining the fiction of their innocence. They knew as well as he did that it was a sham, but it made for less defensive responses and intractable positions. So long as there was pretence, they had no time to consider their answers under any weight of assumed guilt, they had to pretend to be natural. It gave the Inspector a much greater latitude in his approach. As soon as he declared an open attack, they could, without giving grounds for additional suspicion, become extra careful in their responses, wary and guarded. He preferred the present situation.

Talbot had already shown the conventional response to an arrest: denial, non-cooperation, a defensive counter-attack that had been less than fruitful. Perhaps he had been mistaken in arresting him so soon. But there had been pressure from his superiors for action of some sort, and this sop of a bargeman 'detained for questioning' had given him breathing space.

No, on reflection, although the picture was not particularly rosy at the moment, the Inspector felt that he had done the best thing in arresting one element, one piece of the puzzle, and giving the others the illusion of their freedom while letting them know that the bargeman was in custody and under interrogation.

'Those potatoes are for today's lunch,' said Bethan.

The Inspector looked through her. She smiled at him

indulgently and he began wielding the small, sharp knife carefully round the contours of the wet potato in his hand.

Where to go next, though, that was the problem. Potatoes were easy, he could grow good potatoes.

CHAPTER 24

At the Belle Vue, life was returning to an apparent normality: Gertie was once more giving Anna her instructions in the upstairs rooms. And Mary saw her parents together again.

That Sunday lunch-time, for the first time since Beech's disappearance, Gertie walked through the door of the smoke-room and took her place behind the broad counter. One or two of the men tipped their hats and nodded their heads.

When David Riley went to the bar a few minutes later, he inquired after her health with genuine solicitousness. He had always rather liked her; he liked her independence of spirit; he liked the way she smoked her cigarette unashamedly and volunteered her point of view as readily as any of the men present; he thought her attractive and if, as was the rumour, she had been having an affair with the Yorkshireman, so be it. That was a matter for her, for her self-effacing husband and for the opinionated travelling salesman. 'We've missed you, Gertrude. I do hope you're feeling better now.'

'Thank you, David. I'm much better. Some family problems. And then that awful business with . . .'

He relieved her of the difficulty of saying the man's name.

'Of course. A terrible business.' He took his drinks and sat down again.

The atmosphere in the hotel had changed in the last few weeks; the former conviviality in the saloon, the atmosphere that seemed to develop around Beech whenever he had been there, had evaporated. The place was bereft.

Some of the regulars had started to come to the hotel less

often. Others walked past the door and went down to the Greyhound on Waterloo Road instead. They talked about the death of Beech, and they whispered about Gertie's continued absence, but no one suspected for a moment the involvement of the mild-mannered man who stood wiping glasses somnolently behind the bar beyond the glass partition.

They all knew that the silent, rough-looking type who had occasionally been seen in the bar was being questioned about the murder. The rumour was that it was something about buying some drink, an illicit deal that had gone wrong. Beech, trying to make a little killing on the side, had got himself killed. It was only a matter of time, and the bargeman would be charged.

One or two of them pretended to greater knowledge of the criminal than they actually had; claims were made of having stood next to him at the wall in the dark urinal, as if this fact might confer some dubious notoriety upon the speaker; others claimed to have exchanged a 'good evening' or 'good night' with him in the backyard, at the door, or at the bar.

The Inspector played with the food on his plate and Bethan chided him for the waste. She had seen this preoccupied and distracted behaviour before. She tried to sympathize, but couldn't see why he didn't eat his lunch first and then worry.

He offered to help with the washing-up but she declined and he went and sat in the front room at the fireside. Emily played at the table, her house of cards building quietly on the red chenille tablecloth. The Inspector found his place in *The Mayor of Casterbridge* and tried to lose himself in Hardy's description of the well-intentioned but irksome Farfrae. Henchard was the villain, the rough-shod, irrational tyrant, yet one's sympathies were all with him.

In spite of oneself, one loathed the right-thinking, well-intentioned Scotsman, Farfrae. How well Hardy conveyed these contradictions, these paradoxes, thought the Inspector.

He had read all the Wessex novels and re-read his favourites every year. *The Mayor of Casterbridge* he loved most, with its strong, dramatic story, and the tremendous opening with the forlorn couple walking along a desolate road. So many of Hardy's books began thus, he had noticed: a couple, a road, a description of their clothing which told the reader so very much about them, their station, their work. The Inspector knew this particular opening by heart. He particularly admired the detail. Only a close observer could describe so aptly the creases in Michael Henchard's trousers as he shambled along, 'now in the left leg, now in the right'. Hardy would have made a good policeman, thought the Inspector. Self-taught, a keen eye and, most importantly, a tremendous desire to know, always that thirst to know.

He would have to release Talbot. He had held him for three days. There was still no charge. The man showed no sign of weakening. He had questioned him on two more occasions, but the boatman wouldn't budge. He still had the card of little Mary's sighting to play, but it wouldn't be enough on its own. He decided to hold on to it for the time being.

His eyes scanned the same lines again: '*She saw that Donald and Mr Henchard were inseparables. When walking together Henchard would lay his arm familiarly on his manager's shoulder, as if Farfrae were a younger brother, bearing so heavily that his slight figure bent under the weight. Occasionally she would hear a perfect cannonade of laughter from Henchard, arising from something Donald had said, the latter looking quite innocent and not laughing at all.*'

The Inspector pictured only the stern bargeman in his

cell, and Clifford and Gertrude imprisoned in their kitchen. They were all waiting for him. He had to act.

He started at the beginning of the paragraph again, but got no further this time. He laid the book open on his shirt front and closed his eyes as Mary's pile of cards fell quietly down.

He slept fitfully that Sunday night and Bethan showed no good grace to him on Monday morning. 'You were like a whale throwing yourself about in the bed all night. I had to keep trying to get the blankets back. You wrapped them around you, then you started thrashing about and twitching and flinging your arms . . .'

'I'm sorry, love. I slept badly. Things on my mind.'

'Things on my mind too, John. But having no sleep won't help anyone, either Birmingham City Police or Inspector John Hammond's wife and family.'

'No, dear.' And then, plaintively: 'I didn't do it on purpose, you know. I prefer to get a good night's sleep too.' But she was gone, out into the backyard with the washing for the clothes-line.

He would take the attack to them: confront Gertrude and Clifford Benyon with the note and attack Talbot with the sighting by Mary. He would try to panic them into statements that he could then dismember. There was no other way. Talbot would have to be released soon. Today, even. If he had had a solicitor, he wouldn't be in custody now. The man didn't know his rights or, more likely, like most guilty suspects, didn't dare to demand them.

CHAPTER 25

The Inspector knocked at the side door of the Belle Vue. Clifford answered with his shirt sleeves rolled up and collar open, the stud dangling there. 'Good morning, Inspector, Sergeant. What can I do for you?'

'Just a few words, Mr Benyon.' Clifford didn't like the clipped tone.

'Of course. Shall we go upstairs?'

He led the way up the stairs and down the dark, polished linoleum landing into the kitchen.

'Gertie, it's the Inspector. He wants to talk to us again.'

She turned from the sink and looked at the Inspector for a sign, a sign of what this meeting meant. It was an inauspicious time. A Monday morning, the hotel not yet open, the little girl gone to school. She didn't like it.

'Good morning, Inspector. Would you care for a cup of tea, gentlemen?'

The three men sat in awkward silence at the table while Gertrude made tea. The Inspector was content to allow the tense atmosphere to develop and he hoped that Sergeant Preston would have the good sense not to relieve its simmering with small-talk.

Many years ago, an insurance salesman had told the young Inspector (a sergeant himself, then) about what he called 'the period of silence'. After making his sales pitch, outlining his wares, his company's policies, their benefits, the dangers for a young married man with small children of not carrying adequate insurance, should 'the worst' befall him, he outlined the weekly cost, the eventual repayment assuming the survival of the party, the Company's commitment, in the 'tragic event' of an early death, and then he closed his folder, sat back a little in his chair and, most importantly, said not one more word. His theory, and he proved it daily, was that this was the time at which the policy was either bought or rejected. And the choice depended entirely upon who lost the initiative. Whoever broke the hallowed 'period of silence', whoever spoke the next word, had lost the psychological battle. After tense seconds, sometimes minutes, the householder would say something, anything, it didn't matter what, and the salesman knew then that he had won, that he would sell his policy.

Only once had he lost this contest. The would-be client was a retired Welsh farmer. The salesman made his case, closed his folder and sat back. The farmer did the same. The period of silence ensued. And they would still be sitting there now, if the salesman hadn't spoken. For the Welshman had spent his life up on the thin grasslands of Montgomeryshire, with little company but bleating ewes. He was not embarrassed by a few minutes' silence between relative strangers. After nearly five minutes the salesman had been forced to say, 'Well, Mr Jones, what do you think?' And what Mr Jones thought was that he would wait and see.

The Inspector was aware that no matter who relieved the present tension and silence, he had little idea of how he was going to proceed once he began questioning the couple. He felt suddenly rather silly and ill at ease, as if he had no right to be there. His instinct about their guilt, about which he had felt so sure, began to leach from him. Was he barking up the proverbial wrong tree? Did these people have nothing to do with the crime? He could feel the beads of perspiration beginning to gather on his forehead. He was never at his best when he hadn't slept well. Perhaps he shouldn't have come here this morning.

She put the tea in front of the Inspector in a rather challenging, abrupt manner. Did she sense that he was having doubts, losing his confidence? He was losing the initiative, that all-important weapon. The sweat was surely visible on his brow. He reached for his handkerchief and dabbed at his forehead.

They were waiting. They were looking at him. He would have to begin. He exhaled long and deep. Clifford looked at Gertie but she kept her dark eyes on the Inspector and he felt their pressure.

'You know that I have been questioning a man?' The voice was small but not as small as the Inspector had feared. He was judging his performance, his credibility, by their reactions. They seemed to be waiting for more. When it was obvious that this question was awaiting an answer, Clifford looked at Gertie again and said, 'Yes. Yes, you told us you had a suspect, the man from here, I believe.'

'Yes, the man from here. Talbot. Ezra Talbot. He did it, of course.' The Inspector picked up his teacup and it held steady in his hand. It gave him the confidence to try and regain some of the ground that he had felt was slipping away from him. He flashed his eyes at Gertrude, and hers met his. He was aware that his head was submissively bowed. 'He killed Beech. I know this. But I don't think we've been told why.'

Clifford felt the heat inside his boots. He could instantly feel the sticky sweat between his toes. He rubbed them together inside his woollen socks, and they slipped, one against the other.

'I think you need to tell me more about why he killed Beech. I think you have a lot more to tell me.' He looked up, this time bringing up his head as well as his eyes, and looked first at Clifford, where he sensed the greater weakness, and then at Gertrude, who stared back at him and showed no flicker of emotion.

'Could you explain, Inspector? I'm not sure that I follow you,' she said.

He had to admire her. She was going to challenge him head on. God, perhaps she really didn't know. Hadn't suspected the involvement of her own husband. But that was absurd. She was an intelligent woman. She was surely having an affair under his nose. She must know that he could be involved with the killing. But the policeman's confidence was ebbing again. Was he making a most tremendous fool of himself? 'The reason for that man killing Beech is known to all of us sitting here, ma'am.'

'Known to us. What can you mean?' she said. There was a positively haughty tone in her voice.

'Were your relations with Mr Beech all that you have told me, Mrs Benyon? I have reason to believe that they went some way beyond the friendship that you have outlined.'

Clifford glowered across at the policeman. 'Inspector, I cannot let you speak to my wife in that manner. I insist that you withdraw that comment.'

'I'm afraid I can't, Mr Benyon. A man has been killed. I believe that you were involved. And the reason for that involvement was your wife's "friendship" with the deceased.'

Clifford pushed the chair back as he stood and said, 'That's an insulting and disgusting thing to say. I insist that you leave now and that you do not come here again. Unless, of course, you wish to arrest me?'

The Inspector had no intention of leaving, and met the challenging sarcasm with his own measured response. 'Perhaps that can be arranged, Mr Benyon. We'll have to wait and see.'

Clifford, ineptly confident in his position of assumed moral superiority, fired his closing shot: 'And anyway, even if these absurd and offensive lies were true, how on earth do you think that you could prove any such thing?'

The Inspector smiled slowly and warmly at the man

standing across the table from him. He had had few reservations about his involvement, but this crass attempt at open sparring with the professional policeman, a pathetic attempt to assert himself before his wayward wife, merely confirmed it beyond doubt. Clifford had just cooked his goose.

The Inspector drank his tea and asked if there was another drop in the pot. It was the first thing that he had tasted that day.

Now it was only a matter of time. He felt very relieved and wanted to thank Gertie and Clifford for their help and hospitality. However, he simply restricted his comment to a heartfelt, 'What a splendid cup of tea. What is it, Mrs Benyon, Assam?'

It was Darjeeling, but Gertrude felt that the question did not require an answer.

CHAPTER 26

Gertie would have sat tight. Would have met his challenging look with her defiant stare. She knew nothing of crime, but she knew something of men. This man had known nothing. Clifford had told her enough for her to know that it was doubtful that he could have evidence against him. The bargeman was the only danger, and it was unlikely that he was going to confess.

She conjectured correctly. The Inspector was risking all with a little inspired guesswork and the sharp prick of the accusation of infidelity to both husband and wife sitting at their own kitchen table.

And Clifford, who knew nothing of women and, on this showing, as little of men, had just reached up and asked the desperate policeman to hand him down the plaited rope that would surely now snap his neck. She felt indignant. Her affair would now be plastered across the pages of all the Sunday newspapers.

The affection that had flowed back into her while they had sat at this table only two evenings ago, she felt leave her as contempt for his folly negated it. The fool. He didn't deserve her.

Clifford was blurting out the story that he had prepared and outlined to her after the Inspector's last visit: he had been offered some cheap alcohol for the hotel by the bargeman. He had bought some, a small quantity, a few bottles, and sold it from the optics that hung upside down in the bar and saloon. The profit was good and he had bought more. He had shared this secret with Beech, told him that he might buy a few bottles from the itinerant. He knew that the travelling salesman drank a drop, and also that he liked

to give his valued customers a bottle of something now and
again to show his appreciation of their custom. Clifford
assumed that the two men must have met. His own daughter had seen them talking, had she not?

There was a weary tone in the Inspector's voice as he
proceeded to put the obvious questions.

'You are telling me, Mr Benyon, that you shared the
source of your cheap and illicit spirits with a man whom
some people might think you would have no particular
affection for? I know that you contest this view, but I think
that I can substantiate it.' The letter was in his jacket
pocket; it was reassuring.

And why, the Inspector wanted to know, if this were true,
had Clifford told him nothing of it before? Clifford was almost
smug in the neatness of his reply. He was not allowed to buy
spirits for the hotel from anyone but the brewery. This was a
source of their profits and tenants were expected to abide by
this rule. Had he told the police of his doings, the family
would have been put out on the street. They would have lost
their tenancy, their livelihood, their home.

The Inspector was intrigued by this virtuoso performance from the normally reserved Clifford. Naturally, it was
all lies, or at least most of it was lies, but it was fascinating
to see this well-thought-out story, rehearsed who knows
where, polished and reflected upon, until the diffident landlord felt that it would hold up to scrutiny.

And now, it was as if he simply couldn't wait to give his
performance. It was endearing and the Inspector let him
have his head. Benyon embellished a detail here, and gave
a conversation there in his valiant attempt to give the whole
verisimilitude.

Gertrude did not literally raise her eyebrows, but registered such despair in her hollow cheeks and dark eyes that
her response alone would have been enough to convince the
policeman of her husband's lies.

The Inspector turned to Gertrude. 'Is there a drop more tea in the pot, Mrs Benyon, please?'

Gertrude clearly saw through the Inspector's wiles and would have liked to pour the boiling water over his smug head. Instead, she lifted the heavy kettle from the Aga with both hands clasped around its handle, and made a fresh pot of tea.

Clifford felt satisfied with his performance He could no longer feel his toes, they were one sweaty, sticky mass inside his sodden grey socks. But he thought that he had done well. Were they convinced?

The Inspector savoured the tea and played a little waiting game. 'Thank you, Mrs Benyon, delightful.'

'Inspector.' She graciously nodded, with as much loathing for his deft skill as she had contempt for Clifford's mediocrity.

Placing his cup gently on the saucer the Inspector began, 'I wonder, Mr Benyon, when I mention your account of events to the bargeman . . . what's his name . . . ?'

The sergeant ruined this little piece of theatre by interjecting, 'Talbot, sir, Ezra Talbot.'

The Inspector gave him a frosty look, said, 'Thank you, Sergeant,' and echoed the words. 'This bargeman, Ezra Talbot; when I tell him what you have just told me, what do you think that he will have to say?'

Clifford knew that this was where he was likely to have to fight, but he had put all his faith in the notion of *his* word against the other man's. Who would believe an itinerant bargeman who sold stolen spirits, fell out with one of his 'customers' and killed him in a fight, against the word of a respected hotel landlord?

'I think that he might try and implicate me in some way, try and wriggle off the hook himself by trying to blame me, or some other dupe. It's what I would do, wouldn't you, Inspector?'

The effrontery of the man, thought the Inspector, he wants me to play at conspiracy with him. 'Yes, Mr Benyon, I suppose that I might try and blame someone else. And in looking for that someone else, I would try and find someone who had a motive for murder, perhaps a jealous husband, someone whose wife might have given him some heartache, someone whose wife might have been having a relationship with the deceased?'

'I've already told you that you are barking up the wrong tree. You have no evidence for these slurs upon my wife and me. And I would rather that you didn't utter them again.'

The Inspector was rather charmed by this threat. It was like a cornered mouse, instead of running for its hole, standing there and shaking a defiant paw at the marauding cat. 'We'll have to see about that, Mr Benyon.'

It was opening time. There was a distant rattle of the latch at the front door. 'You seem to have a customer, Mr Benyon. And I must be off.'

There was a deceptively jaunty tone in the Inspector's matter-of-fact expression, as if he had overstayed on a social call. But any suggestion of flippancy vanished as he said, 'I'll be coming back later, I'm sure, but for now, if you wouldn't mind, I'd like to leave the sergeant here with you. I'm sure that he'll be as unobtrusive as possible. All right, Preston?'

The sergeant nodded agreement but regretted that he would not be playing dominoes for the White Lion this evening, as arranged.

'If you need anything from the shops, perhaps you could send one of your staff, or your daughter. I think it might be better if you both stayed on the premises, just for the time being, if you don't mind. I'll see myself out, and thank you for the tea, Mrs Benyon. Good morning to you both.'

Almost as an afterthought he turned and walked over to

the sergeant who was still seated at the kitchen table. 'May I?' he said and proffered his hand. The sergeant handed him his little notebook. 'Good day to you both again,' he said and made his way down the dark landing and stairs and out to his car in the October street.

CHAPTER 27

The Inspector skipped up Thornhill Road humming his favourite tune from *Madam Butterfly*. The little dog with its ear cocked to the gramophone spun round in his mind as he hummed along.

It was a lovely autumn evening and the faint glow of yellow light that seeped through from the back kitchen and down the hall on to the front-door glass made him feel most welcome at his own home.

Before he had closed the front door behind him he could smell the cooking cauliflower. Why did cauliflower smell so badly, he wondered. He kissed Emily, and then Bethan, washed his hands at the kitchen sink and went into the garden. 'Where are you going, John?' asked his wife.

He pulled the kitchen door to behind him and wandered up the blue brick path that divided the vegetable beds. The onions had been lifted and plaited and were hanging in the potting shed, the beans had been salted in their jars and the beetroot was bedded down in sand. The ground where they had grown was now rough dug and lay in large, dark clods ready for the winter frosts to break them down.

At the far end of the garden he came to the remaining crops: the four rows of leeks, grown in deference to his mid-Wales wife, and the brassica bed with its leather-leaved plants. The firm sprouts were forming in the stem corners, the cabbages were deeply veined and hearted, and the cauliflowers—those beautiful plants that he grew with such pride, ate with indifference, and smelled cooking with loathing—were developing their creamy hearts amid their peculiarly blue-green leaves. He was well pleased.

Someone had had a garden fire and the smell of the

burning leaves wafted to him. That aria again. When he felt happy, he sang it, or whistled it. He wondered what Mr Giacomo Puccini must have felt that evening in 1864 when he went through to his wife and said, 'Listen to this, Maria. What do you think of this tune I've just written?'

'John . . .' came Bethan's voice from the back kitchen.

'Coming,' he said. 'Coming, love.' But he stayed a few minutes longer, the sprouts at his feet, the faint, tantalizing woody smoke reaching his nostrils, the aria on his lips, and Ezra where he had left him an hour ago in his cell.

He had displayed emotion for the first time. They had sat opposite one another at the table, the Inspector's brown packet of twenty Capstan between them and a note-taking sergeant in the corner by the heavy door with the rectangle of wired glass in it.

The Inspector enjoyed telling the bargeman Clifford's tale. He watched him closely as he gradually parted his lips as the story was unfolded to him. His unsound teeth were yellow and stained. But it was their shape that was revealing. The angle at which both his upper and lower sets protruded gave him a threatening, primæval look which was generally concealed from the world. The Inspector thought of his own collie bitch, Patch, and how her appearance was transformed by the simple expedient of lifting back her upper lip. In this instant Patch, the docile collie, was metamorphosed into its near-relative, the pack wolf; the pet dog looked suddenly and alarmingly an impostor at the domestic fireside. And here, across the table from the Inspector, was that same predator.

Ezra listened in silence. He rolled a thin cigarette as the Inspector continued to observe him. As he drew in the blue smoke his lips concealed his teeth, as he exhaled, the beast was revealed. The story went on. The cigarette was extinguished roughly in his fingers, smudged out and dropped to the floor. The lips parted wider. This was the face that Beech must have last seen, thought the Inspector as he watched the effect of his every word.

Ezra was hearing a story that he knew *could* be true. That white-faced fool Clifford was trying to frame him. But why? They had been safe. The police had no evidence. Why had he given in? But if they were undone, he would take the other man with him, the landlord must know this.

Perhaps it was a ruse, a last shot of the Inspector's. He had grasped at some information, and he was trying a bluff. That must be it.

The Inspector finished. He leaned back in the creaking bentwood chair. Its broken glue joints rocked ominously beneath his pressure. He lit a cigarette and pushed the open packet towards his adversary. The other man did not look down.

'You're making this up. I never killed anyone. This land-lord's got it in for me. *He* must've done it if he's come this with you. Or you're making the whole thing up. You've got nothing and you're trying to pin it on me. Get some bloke off the cut, someone who no one'll bother about and pin it on them. Not me. Not Ezra Talbot. You know nothing.'

The Inspector took Preston's notebook from inside his worsted jacket pocket, thumbed through the pages until he found the place that he was looking for, and then carefully tipped his ash to the floor. He bent the page back and pushed it across to Ezra. The bargeman looked at the hiero-glyphics and stared back at the Inspector blankly.

'You can't read?' said the policeman considerately. Ezra nodded his head. 'Sergeant—' the Inspector beckoned the man in the corner. He laid his own pad down and came to the table. 'Read it, please.'

The young man began at the top of the page, '. . . reckon Talbot arranged to meet Beech in his barge that evening to buy some. There must have been an argument, something to do with the drink. He must have killed him. It was the last time I saw him alive.' The Inspector raised his finger and the sergeant returned to his seat. 'I think he's done for you, Ezra, don't you?'

The man was still unsure. He needed time to think. Was this a trap that he couldn't see? Beware haste. Any sudden words could put him on the gallows. 'I don't believe it. I don't believe you. I'm saying nothing.'

The Inspector guessed that he was playing for time. That was all right by him. He had time.

'Good night, Talbot. We'll see what a night's sleep does for you. But don't forget, it's your neck.'

For three days after the policeman had questioned him, William loitered about the wharf. He had little money, but on the second day he had managed to earn fifteen shillings unloading a flour barge of its unwieldly sacks. By five that afternoon his back ached from the great, lifeless sacks and his face and hair were pasty, dusty white from the flour. As he shuffled back along the wharf, some urchin boat children jeered at his ghostly visage, but he sneered at them, and they stopped immediately.

He had no idea how long the police would hold his employer, but he didn't think it could be much longer now. It didn't occur to him that Ezra might be guilty. A murderer was someone different, not that gloomy man whom he had towed up and down the cuts of central England for the last ten years. That man didn't murder people. When they had heard the news of the body in the cut when they were up near Tarporley, Ezra had been as interested as anyone else, but no more so.

The police were always after the boat people: thieving, fighting, the odd arson attack between rival carriers, these things were common enough. But murder was rare. William knew no murderers. Ezra would be out soon, and they could get going again. This hanging around the wharf was worse than walking the cut. And it paid nothing.

The next morning, the Inspector was whistling. Bethan would be glad when he finally breezed out of the house. The man had no middle ground: if he wasn't preoccupied and worried and puzzling over some case, he was euphoric

and singing or whistling. He was not at all like the steady
men that she had known in Newtown, before she had fallen
for this clever policeman from Birmingham on a cycling
holiday in Wales all those years ago.

He knew that today Talbot would break. He would have
had long enough to consider his options. His conspirator
was trying to send him to the gallows. He would clutch
at the straw of making a confession. Could he avoid the
threatening rope if he told all? He would draw close across
the table, conspiratorially close and wail like a child as he
saw the dark doors around him closing.

The Inspector would listen. Make no promises. Say that
he would see what he could do. It would be best if the man
told him everything. There would be another delay, and
then he would confess. The Inspector would hear the detail,
the bits of detail that he loved to know. Why, and where,
and how, and with whom.

He parked the black Austin in Colmore Circus and strode
up Steelhouse Lane to the station. He pushed open the
heavy oak doors and stopped humming.

The man walking towards him was George Matlock, of
Matlock, Airey and Brown. He knew him well enough.
'Good morning, Inspector,' said the solicitor.

'Hello, Matlock,' said the Inspector as he looked him up
and down, surveying the dark jacket and formal striped
trousers.

'You have a Mr Talbot in custody, I believe? I would
like to know whether he has been charged with any offence?
If not, whether you intend to charge him? How long has he
been in custody, and how long do you intend to detain him?
I would like to see him as soon as possible.' He was civil,
distant, assured, and wholly correct.

The Inspector was crestfallen. He had nothing tangible.
But he knew that given a little longer, he would have had
a confession. Of course it was the man's right to have legal

representation. Of course he shouldn't hold him this long
without a charge being brought. But God knows, if the
public didn't want the streets thronged with criminals, the
police had to bend the regulations a little now and then.
He wasn't talking of beating people, forcing confessions out
of them. All he wanted was a little time, the creation of a
little duress. Not much more than a parent had to apply to
a child before it would own up to scrumping or breaking a
vase.

'Who called you in, Matlock?' asked the Inspector. The
two men had known one another for some years. They were
not friends, but they respected one another.

Matlock's reply was courteous and puzzled. 'I'm not in
a position to tell you, Inspector. As a matter of fact, I
don't know. I received in the first post this morning an
instruction, and an adequate sum to cover it. It simply
asked me to ensure that the detained man was aware of his
rights. Is he?'

While the solicitor was ensconced with Talbot, the Inspector was in the Chief Constable's office on the first floor
of the building. 'I haven't got enough. He did it. I know,
and he knows I know. The landlord put him up to it. I
don't know for how much, but that's the way of it. Another
day, two at the most, and I'd have had the killer and a
confession from him that Benyon put him up to it. It would
all fall into place. But at the moment, I haven't got a thing.
Nothing to hold him with.'

Half an hour later, the two men stood at the window and
looked down as Talbot left through the front doors at Matlock's side. They stood on the pavement for a few minutes.
The bargeman's face was expressionless. The solicitor
talked to him at the same time as he looked up and down
Steelhouse Lane. And then, with a small punctilious bow
of the head he hailed a passing taxi.

Talbot watched the solicitor step into the rear of the car
and then, with his hands deep in his trouser pockets, he
walked off down the hill.

CHAPTER 29

All the feelings of grief that Gertie had experienced at the disappearance of Beech, and the eventual knowledge of his murder, had turned to contempt for her foolish husband, who had now surely implicated himself in the crime by trying to frame Talbot. She had returned to her own bedroom, and although she was serving in the saloon once more, they barely acknowledged one another in private. They knew that another visit from the Inspector was imminent, and they feared the worst.

Clifford was drowning. The Inspector had made plain his contempt for the story of Talbot, the liquor and Beech. Clifford regretted being unable to share with him the irony of how very near the truth it actually was. And now Gertie was ridiculing his folly in thinking that the police would be so much more inclined to believe a publican than an itinerant bargeman.

With his suspect released, the Inspector was dejected. He loathed the idea of the guilty man escaping. It happened. But not usually when the identity of that guilty man was known to the police and others. There was always a slip, always a bit of evidence that could be found. But here, this man was now going to escape justice. It irked the Inspector. He whistled no airs now.

He had to call on the couple. The sergeant was still there; he and a constable had been taking shifts and maintaining a discreet presence on the premises. He waited until closing time in the afternoon and approached the door as Clifford was about to bolt it.

'Inspector,' said the landlord.

'Mr Benyon. Can I have a word with you and your wife, please?'

It wasn't right. Clifford didn't know what was coming. But there was something in the Inspector's tone which was not right. His wife had told him that it was only a matter of time and they would surely come and take him away. They would smear her in the court and the press would revile her. *She* would be seen as the guilty one by the petty-minded Birmingham bourgeoisie with their fine houses and net curtains and jealous envy. Clifford's fate was decided. But she would be seen as the guilty woman.

He called Gertie from the saloon and she stood at the doorway, defiant. 'Inspector,' she said, by way of curt greeting.

The policeman told them that he had released his suspect. 'The guilty man has gone free, for the time being. There has been a miscarriage of justice here, as you two well know. But, for the moment, there is no more that I can say or do. Good day.' The sergeant got up from his seat by the window and walked out of the hotel with him. The Inspector asked him to take the car, he would walk. He would see him back at the station later on.

The couple were intrigued, but they did not discuss this development. They saw it as a temporary respite, no more. She returned to the saloon, finished her tidying and then passed her husband in silence as she went up to her room to rest.

Clifford stayed at the bar and drank a large whisky. He had got Talbot out of custody, but he knew that he didn't have long. It would only be a matter of time before one or the other of them were questioned again and further police pressure applied.

While the matter of Ezra exercised his lurching mind, it was his relationship with Gertie which pained him. Briefly he had had her again. She had been his wife once more. He was frantic to keep her. Two nights ago he had ground his loins against her dark pelvic bone in an agony of passion for her. She had been listless with fatigue and racked by recent grief, but he had felt once more her nascent love.

Afterwards, they had lain on their backs, side by side, their fingers lightly intertwined. He had resolved then never to lose her again. For the love of her, he had had a man killed. To save his own skin he had tried to sacrifice the killer to the police. And now, to save their love, he would kill the killer himself.

While Gertie rested in her room, Clifford went to the shed that abutted the Gents and examined his old bicycle. He hadn't ridden it since the day it was pushed into the shed along with the lawn-mower, tea chests, a wooden crate of hand tools, a tray of chisels, and tins of grease, nails and screws.

It was very dusty and the rear tyre needed air but, apart from this, it was in much the same condition as it had been when they had first moved in two years ago. He pumped up the tyre, felt the edges with his thumb and fingers, and screwed the valve-cap back on. He wiped the leather saddle clean and pulled from a tea chest an old, dark blue linen coat.

Before going back upstairs, he dipped his finger into a tin of yellow grease and, looking about the yard and then up at the windows, he walked to the side gate and smeared a dab on to each of the hinges. He drew the gate to him and it let out a squeak. But, as the grease penetrated, and he pushed the gate from him once more, it was silent.

CHAPTER 30

At closing time that night, as he cleaned up alone in the
bar below, he heard Gertrude walk along the landing and
go straight to her room. He turned off the lights in the pub
and went upstairs to his room, where he sat on the edge of
the bed in the dark, the door slightly ajar.

In ten minutes she came out of her room and went along
the landing again, this time to the bathroom. All his senses
were alive to her every movement. He heard her slip the
little brass bolt and then, a few minutes later, break wind.
He smiled. A few minutes more and there came the sound
of the chain being pulled, the seat cover lowered, the tap
running, and then the sound of the cold water tap and the
noisy cistern refilling while she cleaned her teeth. The
sound of the bolt slipping back and the door opening, the
gushing and gurgling of the water-closet as it filled to the
top, and then her quiet glide down the landing to her bedroom, the door of which she closed quietly behind her.

He turned down his bed, ruffled up the blankets and
made a half-hearted attempt to create a shape beneath the
covers. No one would come in, but just in case. His shoes
in his hands, he tiptoed down the landing and stairs and
out through the pub into the yard.

He drew out his cycle and checked the tyre. It was still
inflated. He pulled the short dark coat over his shirt and
trousers, buttoned it up and tucked his trousers into his
socks.

With the cycle leaning against the wall, its front wheel
pointing into the shed, he clicked the dynamo on, lifted the
rear wheel and brought his sole down on the pedal. A flicker
of light played on the trays of tools on the rough-hewn

shelves at the far end. As the light faded, he reached to what he had seen and took in his hand a one-inch chisel from among the pliers and snips, files and bradawls.

He left by the quiet side gate, the little smears of grease glistening on the hinges. He was aware of the absurdity of the spectacle that he must present, and it was to Gertie that his thoughts turned. If she could see him now, gliding past Five Ways, along Islington Row and down the back streets to avoid the city centre, the cycle swishing along the dry silent roads, the fat chisel in his pocket knocking against his thigh.

He came over the hump-backed bridge and silently scooted down among the moored barges. What was its name? Talbot had mentioned it, but Clifford was hopeless with names. It was something predatory. *Eagle* or *Bear*. He hoped he would know it, that the name would trigger his memory.

Some were empty, and many didn't have accommodation, they were just flat, cargo-carrying hulks. But quite a number did, and he needed to approach with great care. Now he pushed the cycle quietly along the wharf. He knew nothing of boats or barges, he'd never looked at them this closely before. There was a little light from the sky, a few stars, and glimpses of glancing moon from behind the clouds.

He came to some cranes and lifting tackle. He continued. Fifty yards further down the wharf, which was here no more than a wide towpath with a single railway line abutting it, there were a few barges moored away from the main commercial base.

There she was. The first one of the stragglers that he came to. The name was *Crow*. There was no doubt. This was the one.

He saw a shape in the distance ascend and then descend

the hump-backed bridge. It didn't appear on the wharf and must have continued down the road. He waited to make sure.

The boat was silent. There was no movement. Was that the faintest skein of smoke leaking from the chimney? He stood the cycle against one of the neat piles of timber pit-props that stood beside the path and walked to the edge of the dark water.

Making himself have no weight, he stepped carefully aboard. The boat barely moved beneath him. He stood in the hatch with his eyes shut tight; he waited longer, longer. He wanted to open them. He was bursting with a desire to look; there was a humming of the enormous silence in his ears but he held his eyes tight shut.

When he opened them, it was as if to half light. He squinted and could see clearly the things about him. He pressed up to the crack at the top of the hatch doors. There was the man, sleeping. He put a finger into the crack and eased a door back towards him an inch. It gave, it was open. He drew out the chisel and pulled his blue collar about him, right to his neck. He opened both doors at once and took a step on to the cabin floor. As he lifted his right hand all the way back it hit the cabin roof, and that little noise caused the sleeper to stir. He half-turned as Clifford brought down the chisel. Even with this force behind it, he felt a little catch as it met the woollen blanket. But it was only for a fraction of a second and then the chisel hit bone and out it came and in again and sank into soft flesh and then broke small bone and the shape beneath the cover writhed in pain and shock and moved obligingly, offering itself again and again: buttocks, breast, thigh, waist, shoulder, up and down the arm came, in and out the square, sharp, rusty end plunged. Until all was still. And the only sound was of Clifford's gasping breathing.

CHAPTER 31

It was Saturday lunch-time and Aston Villa were playing at home. They had started well: played nine, won six and drawn three. The winger, Houghton, was roasting right-backs up and down the country. The streets around Lozells Road were thronged with crowds as forty thousand followers headed towards Villa Park.

Walking against this crowd, heading towards the city centre and Nechells Wharf, was the big, stooped figure of Ezra Talbot. Talbot had never been to a football match, thought the notion of football as silly as he thought other games were. His eyes hardly looked up at the passing crowds as they streamed down the Soho Road, past Villa Cross and finally down the long straight of Trinity Road which brought them their first sight of the red-brick, Victorian pillared edifice that was their team's home.

The Inspector moped about the house. He wandered in the garden, read a little in the front room, pottered about the kitchen, all the time getting in Bethan's way as she baked and cleaned. In despair, she finally asked him if Villa were playing at home today. He hadn't even thought of it. Yes, of course they were. They were playing Chelsea. Dark blue against Villa's elegant claret and blue. He would go. He'd leave now and walk. Perhaps have a pint of beer on the way. He picked up his old jacket, stuffed a cap into the pocket, patted his waistcoat for his cigarettes and walked down the entry into the street.

By Villa Cross at half past two, he was borne along by the sheer volume of the buoyant crowd. In the noisy, good-natured mob his thoughts drifted back to the case. He wondered what he could have done that would have prevented that slippery eel Talbot from escaping his grasp. No doubt he was very pleased to be out of custody and half way safe, but he was doubtless also full of bitterness and rancour against the mild-mannered landlord who had embroiled him in the murder in the first place, and then abandoned him to the police.

Talbot would want to level that score, of this the Inspector was certain. He didn't know when, or how, but level it he surely would.

Outside the pork butcher's, half way down Lozells Road, the two men passed one another. Both solitary figures within a huge crowd, each thinking of the other, and each wholly unaware of the proximity of his adversary.

From the bridge Talbot could see that *Crow* had been moved. He expected as much. She would have obstructed other vessels' unloading. There was a small crowd at the far end. She would probably be there. He entered the wharf and approached. There were police. A car was drawn up and there were two constables fronting the children and the little crowd who were bearing down on the barge. It was *Crow*. He pushed his way to the front and told the constables that it was his boat. The policeman looked him up and down and nodded him through. As he passed, the constable called, 'Sarge!' and the sergeant at the water's edge met him. 'What do you want?' he asked gruffly.

'It's my boat. What's going on?'

'What's your name?'

'Talbot. Ezra Talbot. What's going on here. It's my boat.'

The policeman nodded him aboard. 'Don't go in. And don't touch anything.' Ezra stepped aboard. He pulled open the hatch doors and could see beneath the grey blanket the twisted shape of something. The blanket was stained with dark patches and the floor had large pools of dried blood on it. One of William's dirty black boots was lying on the floor, a string in it for a lace. The cabin was hot. A big, lazy bluebottle zoned around aimlessly.

The scene was uncannily like the one that he had himself perpetrated. This was a body. He was not being played with, was he? This was not some elaborate hoax dreamt up by that wily Inspector, was it? He knew it could not be. The way that the body lay there. It was dead. Of that he had no doubt.

Not one thought or feeling passed through his mind for the deceased. He had no sense of sorrow, regret or sadness. Just an idle curiosity. Not entirely idle, though. The one thing, apart from the shape on the floor, that caught his eye was the unusual padlock and key that sat on the shelf above the bunk. It was new. William must have bought it. He'd broken the old one off to get on board to sleep. And it had cost him his life. Expensive lock, smiled Ezra to himself.

At Villa Park, the central defender, Gibson, got his first goal of the season and Astley, the talented outside-right, scored two. The Villa won, three-one. The Inspector found himself involved sporadically. He applauded the goals, the good passes, the winning tackles, but only with the prompting of those about him. Without their cue, the players would have had neither Hammond's support nor censure. At twenty to five, and with a hint of dusk in an orange October sky, he joined the throng that once more snaked through the streets of Aston and Perry Barr.

There was a message for him on the hall table where the newspaper and post were always left. It had come by hand and was from the Superintendent. '*John, come to Steelhouse Lane immediately, Richard.*'

*

The Superintendent briefed his inspector. Yes, naturally they'd brought in Talbot. But the man wasn't stupid, or psychopathic, as far as the Superintendent knew. He wouldn't kill his hired man and then return as if he'd never been there. He said he had an alibi. Been with that whore he visits. 'Went straight to her when he was released from here. Been with her all night, he says. His lad had been dead for at least twelve hours according to the doctor. Some barge kids found him, playing around and saw the open doors. Very nasty. Big wounds. Sharp, square implement, the doctor reckons, a chisel or screwdriver probably. Horrible mess. I've got someone round with the woman now, checking her story. If she's lying, we'll find out. But it doesn't add up. What's going on, John? The Chief Constable's not going to like this. One canal murder, the main suspect set free, is one thing. Two—what's the saying?—something about being careless.'

'Yes. Oscar Wilde I think, sir. Something like that anyway.'

The Inspector didn't like it either. He would speak to Ezra, but he was out of the question as a suspect. Why would someone kill William? Had the Inspector missed something? Did the young lout know more than he had let on? Or did someone *think* he did? The Inspector was quietly excited; the case was on the boil again. This morning it was a rapidly dying duck. Now it was alive again, and this time there would be no released suspects. 'I'll go down and talk to the bargeman,' he said.

'All right. Keep me informed. And John . . .'

'Yes,' said the Inspector, as he stood at the door.

'How did the lads get on?'

'I think they won,' said Hammond, as he pulled the door to behind him.

CHAPTER 32

The Inspector stood in the doorway. Talbot's alibi had been established by his woman in Silas Square. And anyway, unless the Inspector was more wrong than he cared to be, there was no motive for him killing his hired hand. Ezra was only going to commit one murder in his lifetime, and he'd already done it.

The tone was almost friendly, the Inspector's manner relaxed. In the bentwood chair he stretched his legs out and crossed his feet. When he offered Ezra a cigarette he proffered the packet in his hand, all the way to the other man's hand. He dismissed the sergeant who had been seated in the corner when he had entered.

'This talk is between you and me, Ezra.'

It was the first time that the Inspector had used the killer's forename.

'It's off the record. We both know things that others don't. The time's right to share our knowledge, for both our sakes. Who killed your man?'

'God knows. I went back this morning and someone had topped him.'

'Who'd want to kill him?'

'I did, sometimes. Lazy bastard,' answered Ezra.

What a difference, the Inspector thought, between a man telling the truth, even to an admission of this sort, and the guarded, wary answers of the same man earlier when he had clearly been involved with the crime.

'Are you telling me you killed him?' asked the Inspector ingenuously.

'Of course I didn't, you know that. Why would I want

to kill the little runt? I said I *could've* killed him. Many's the
time. I never liked him. I won't say I did.'

'So who wanted him dead?'

'I dunno.'

'Maybe it wasn't your man they wanted to kill. Maybe
it was you. You saw the body, a mess I know, not that
that will have surprised you.' He couldn't avoid the cheap,
knowing aside, but it was foolish to antagonize the man in
this way and he hurried on: 'The body was covered, the
man was asleep. Whoever did it may not have known that
it wasn't you he killed.'

'And who wants me dead?'

'We know who wants you dead, Ezra. Someone who
thinks that you're a liability, a risk. Someone who knows
that you might have something on him that you're not
prepared to forget, especially after what that person did, or
tried to do. Think about it. What would you have done in
his place? There's no need to answer. Just think about it.'

CHAPTER 33

While Talbot was sitting across from the Inspector, Clifford Benyon was accompanying the sergeant and a constable to the police station. The Inspector had told them to say nothing of the nature of the current inquiry and to summon him from the interview room as soon as the landlord arrived at the station.

As he left home Clifford had kissed little Mary who walked with him down to the street and saw him step into the black car where she had revealed her important piece of information to the friendly Inspector a few days ago.

She kissed her father back and asked him when he would be coming home. 'Soon, Mary. Soon, I hope.'

As the car pulled away, Clifford looked back at Mary on the kerb and saw through the open gate the wheel of his bicycle sticking slightly out of the shed where he had pushed it last night.

As soon as the black car pulled into the yard at the rear of the police station, the Inspector was called down from the second floor to meet him.

'Mr Benyon,' said the Inspector, and led the way along the corridor and then up the first broad staircase.

Clifford walked slowly through the alien surroundings. The glossy green paint made him feel slightly bilious. There was the sound of male voices echoing from distant parts of the building. The Inspector walked a step ahead of the publican in silence.

On the second floor, they turned right and walked past a door marked 'Interview Room'. It had a number. It was empty.

The second one they passed had someone in it. The

Inspector paused and nodded his head slightly towards the glass panel. As Benyon peered in the Inspector rapped the door sharply with his knuckle. Talbot spun round in his seat and the two men's eyes met.

Clifford started to pour with sweat. His legs folded beneath him. There was the man that he had killed last night. He had stabbed him a dozen times. And now, there he sat.

With the sergeant's help he faltered along to the next room and was ushered in. The Inspector leaned on the window-sill and lit a cigarette. Clifford cradled his head in his hands and the sergeant sent the constable for some hot tea. As the sweat poured from him, Clifford loosened his tie and removed his jacket. His feet were wet inside his sodden woollen socks.

He asked that he might use the toilet. The Inspector nodded agreement. The sergeant walked with him down the corridor. Clifford was barely in control of his legs as he walked with one hand trailing along the painted wall.

Inside the cool, echoing room, Clifford pointed to the door of a WC. The policeman stepped outside.

After five minutes he came back into the lavatory and saw the door of the cubicle into which Clifford had gone slightly ajar. There was something on the floor. He could see the boots. He pushed open the door as far as it would go. The weight was great and there was the thud of the slightly bumping body. The man was still moving, but they were death throes. His neck had been broken as he had stepped from the lavatory bowl and now, cruelly and horribly, the thin strong cord from his boots was cutting deep into his neck and throat. His face was disfigured, his frothy tongue hanging from his colourless lips.

The sergeant wrestled with the inert body, but Clifford's weight had knotted the thin cord too tightly on the big coat hook and he could not move him. He called down the corridor and the young constable who had brought the tea now fumbled out his pocket knife and cut down his first suicide, before he was sick on to the floor.

The Inspector stood above the corpse in the echoing urinal and saw himself defeated. He pulled the lavatory door to him and looked at the cord where it had been cut. The scene reminded him of those pages in *Jude the Obscure* where Hardy has the stunted boy 'Little Father Time' destroy himself in this way. It had never read satisfactorily to the Inspector. There was something uncharacteristically surreal about the incident. But here, in a police station in Birmingham on a Saturday evening in October, was a similar death for entirely different reasons.

With his hands folded behind his head and his legs stretched out once more beneath the table, the Inspector asked the bargeman, 'How much did you do it for, Talbot?' He didn't expect an answer, of course.

Talbot looked back at him. Was he mad? Did he expect a reply?

'Did he still owe you some? It's the usual arrangement in these matters. Half before, half after. But I can tell you, you won't be getting any more out of him. He's just hanged himself. Careless of us. We had him. Would have got him for last night's business and then we'd have had you too. You've been lucky. Very lucky. You came that close—' The Inspector put his thumb and forefinger within an inch of one another.

'Get out.' Hammond tapped at his cigarette packet, rolled it round and round on the table, round tap tap, round tap tap. 'Go on, you're free to go, get out of here.'

Talbot left the room and was escorted down the two flights of stairs and into the street by a constable.

The Inspector stood at the window and watched him

until he eventually lost him in the Saturday evening crowds on Corporation Street, ordinary people out for a drink, on their way to a dance, or coming from the pictures, a quiet murderer in their midst.